All's Fair in Love and Rodeo

All's Fair in Love and Rodeo

Grit and Grace Romance

Leah Vale

TULE
PUBLISHING

All's Fair in Love and Rodeo
Copyright© 2024 Leah Vale
Tule Publishing First Printing, August 2024

The Tule Publishing, Inc.

ALL RIGHTS RESERVED

First Publication by Tule Publishing 2024

Cover by Lee Hyat Designs

No part of this book may be used or reproduced in any manner whatsoever without written permission except in the case of brief quotations embodied in critical articles and reviews.

This is a work of fiction. Names, characters, places, and incidents are products of the author's imagination or are used fictitiously. Any resemblance to actual events, locales, organizations, or persons, living or dead, is entirely coincidental.

AI was not used to create any part of this book and no part of this book may be used for generative training.

ISBN: 978-1-964418-25-4

Dedication

For Terri Reed, "What if" partner extraordinaire.
And Sinclair Jayne, for steering my "What ifs" in the right direction.

Dear Reader,

One of my favorite fantasies (don't worry, it's not spicy) is to live and work on a rodeo rough stock ranch, and a perk of being a romantic fiction author is having the chance to bring that fantasy to life. And getting to work in my pajamas, of course. All's Fair in Love and Rodeo is the first book in my Grit and Grace series featuring a group of women who trade in their competitive rodeo ranch bronc riding chaps for a partnership raising and training the animals used in rodeos.

Tasked with securing their first rodeo contract, Samantha "Sammie" Abel is shocked when the handsome cowboy she'd ghosted shows up on their ranch intent on winning the same contract.

Almost as shocked as Alec Neisson is when he finds out why she'd left him without so much as a goodbye.

The women of Grit and Grace are determined to make it in a man's world, but unexpectedly find love along the way.

Prologue

Pineville, Oregon

"WE'VE BEEN *CANCELED!*"

Samantha "Sammie" Abel gripped the edge of the tall table they'd gathered around and closed her eyes against the refrain the other four women had seemingly been taking turns repeating. While she might be able to shut out the volume of Emma Berrett's delivery, easily heard over the live country rock band performing in the Ninth Chute Dance tent, Sammie couldn't shut out the impact of the words.

"Maybe that's not what she meant," Beth Dawson said, hope bright in her dark eyes. Ever the optimist.

Laura Senske set her beer down hard. "Come on, Beth. Natalie's exact words were, *Sorry ladies, but we've been canceled. Pack your saddles and find your way home.* What else could she have meant?"

Meira Ware leaned her elbows on the table and slowly turned her untouched beer. "I don't even have a home right now. I broke my lease when I was cast on the show."

The constriction in Sammie's throat tightened. She had a home in Texas. But it was owned and occupied by her grandmother, Barbara "Babs" Abel. The woman whose idea of successfully raising a young girl was to tell her she'd never amount to anything and constantly reminding her it was a good thing she's pretty. But Sammie had found ranch saddle bronc riding, faking it until she was making it, and Buckin' TV had found her. As a Buckin' Babe she'd been on her way to amounting to something, all right.

Emma tossed her long, platinum-blonde hair over her shoulder. "What about the contracts we signed? We have three months left on them. How can they just cut us loose? How could Natalie do that to us?"

The business wiz of the bunch, Laura sighed. "You didn't read the fine print, did you? The network retained the right to sever the agreement at any time. As Executive Producer of *Buckin' Babes*, Natalie was simply doing her job."

Fighting the fear threatening to strangle her, Sammie cast her gaze around the tent, the growing post-rodeo crowd illuminated by strings of small lights draped over their heads and the spotlights shining on the band. She caught sight of Dan, the cameraman for the small reality-ish *Buckin' Babes* TV crew. He was staggering through the crowd with a beer bottle in one hand and a large shot glass filled with brown liquor in the other. Had he been cut loose too?

He spotted their glum group standing around one of the tall tables ringing the dance floor and made his way to them.

Sammie greeted him with a nod.

"Ladies," he said in return.

In unison they said, "Dan."

Sammie asked, "Do you know if the network pulled the plug on the whole *Buckin' Babes* show or—" Her voice caught. "Or just this cast?"

"The whole show. Lock, stock, and buckin' barrel." He tossed back the shot of what Sammie could now smell to be whiskey. Gesturing around the table with the empty glass, he said, "You all are lucky. You're pretty, so you'll be just fine."

It's a good thing you're pretty.

Sammie clenched her jaw against the painful echo of her grandmother's words. *The prettier you are, the easier it'll be to trap a man.* Heaven forbid a guy would want her for what was on the inside.

The way the other Buckin' Babes straightened away from the high table, sending each other dark looks, told Sammie they felt the same way she did about Dan's comment.

Clueless, he saluted them with the glass and wandered away toward the long, crowded bar set up at the far end of the tent.

Laura grumbled, "I used to like him."

Everyone nodded in agreement. Though they were all very different, these women had become real friends as they traveled around the west, putting on exhibitions of ranch saddle bronc riding.

"Eff that," Emma said. "We are so much more than the

way we look."

The determination that had driven Sammie to leave her grandmother's vitriol behind and join the women's bronc riding circuit in Texas surged through her. "There is nothing these cowboys can do that we can't."

"Except ride bulls," Meira interjected.

"Speak for yourself," Peyton Halliday said, appearing out of seemingly nowhere, wedging her petite frame between Meira and Laura. The fiery redhead was a thrill seeker extraordinaire and would have happily taken a crack at riding a bull.

At least until she'd met Dr. Drew Neisson, grandson of Thomas Wright. Sammie had encouraged Peyton to wrap the good doc around her finger, but he'd turned the tables and was putting a ring on hers. Not that Peyton needed the financial security, but she'd be set for life after she became part of the Wright Ranch rodeo roughstock dynasty.

A light bulb went off in Sammie's head. "You guys, listen. We should start our own rodeo roughstock company."

They stared at her as if she'd landed on her head in the arena one time too many.

"No, just listen to me. Beth, the stock love you—"

"Except for sheep. No sheep, please," Beth said. To generate content for the *Buckin' Babes* show, Beth and Peyton had attempted to ride the sheep meant for the children's mutton-busting contest. Needless to say, the attempt hadn't gone well.

Sammie laughed. "Okay, no sheep. And Emma, you're not afraid of anything. You can help Beth with the training. Laura, Miss MBA, you'll obviously handle the business. And Meira—good lord—we've got a gold mine in you with all that science-y stuff you used to do."

Meira arched a reddish-brown brow. "You mean genetic research?"

"Yes. That." Sammie was definitely getting fired up about the idea. Hope made her cheeks flush with heat. She might not have to say goodbye to this amazing group of friends, after all. "And I'll handle getting us the rodeo contracts."

"You'll double-dog dare them?" Peyton asked knowingly.

Sammie winked. Convincing people to do things was her superpower.

Laura asked, "There's just the small matter of a large enough ranch and the seed money to buy the bulls, and broncs, and steers . . ."

Peyton, of the oil billionaire Hallidays, grinned. "I think I can help with that."

There was a moment of silence as the women contemplated Sammie's outrageous proposal.

Sensing that all they needed was a nudge, Sammie said gently, "We'll never know unless we try."

Laura straightened. "Why the hell not?"

Talking all at once, her friends agreed that they did indeed have a plan for their future, that they could take control and find a way to thrive in the very manly man's world of rodeo roughstock contracting. The constriction in Sammie's throat eased and happiness spread through her.

A deep voice she recognized said right next to her ear, "Hey, tough stuff, how about a dance?"

His words settled deep in her belly. Sammie's smile widened and she turned into his arms, meeting the heat in his blue, blue eyes. "Why not?"

Chapter One

"Wait a second. My spur's come undone," Emma said.

Sammie pulled up and stopped next to Emma at the base of the metal stairs leading to the raised platform above the practice chute. Emma flipped her chaps aside and knelt on one knee to buckle her spur and pull it tight over her dusty, well-worn cowboy boot.

"This strap is about shot," Emma groused.

Stating the obvious, Sammie said, "You need new spurs."

Emma kept her focus on the spur strap, clearly trying to force the buckle to fasten on the hole in the leather that wasn't cracked nearly all the way through. "We all need a lot of things, but if I screw up today, we'll have to learn to do without."

"You won't screw up. You're good at this."

As Emma switched legs to re-buckle her other spur, Sammie pulled in a calming lungful of the crisp May morning air and shifted her gaze to the seemingly endless view beyond the slight knoll that the A Bar H Ranch structures had been built on. Ancient live oaks and black hickory trees gave way to grasslands speckled with exposed granite. The land here was beautiful.

The Texas Hill Country was perfect. The A Bar H Ranch was perfect. Ripe for success. A perfect place for the birth of the Grit and Grace Rodeo Roughstock Company. Among other things.

Sammie's gaze drifted past the chute and out over the corral to the groups of men—potential investors, but still just men—talking to each other outside the high, metal corral fence. They were dressed in varying degrees of cowboy casual, ranging from western-style shirts, jeans, and boots to lightweight suits, bolo ties, and boots. The cowboy hats were a necessity beneath the already hot July Texas sun. Ten deep pockets and their representatives had accepted the invitation extended by the former Buckin' Babes.

Maybe just out of curiosity. Sammie shouldn't care why they'd traveled to the high-end ranch she and her friends were lucky enough to call theirs just outside of Last Stand, Texas. The women had been able to lease the huge property for a fraction of its value, thanks to Peyton.

Peyton's oldest brother, Asher Halliday, had bought the ranch, changing the name to A Bar H, as an investment and updated it to an oil billionaire's standards. But for whatever reason, Asher had lost interest in the place and had been willing to lease it to his sister's friends for a song. Most of the rough stock—bucking bulls, broncs, and steers—that hadn't already been here at the A Bar H were coming to them courtesy of Peyton's new fiancé, Drew Neisson, in two weeks' time. More specifically, they were coming from Drew's grandfather, Thomas Wright, of the renowned Wright Ranch. A legend in the rodeo roughstock game.

Though why the Wright Ranch would want to supply a future competitor with bulls and broncs, even clear down here in the Texas circuit, was beyond Sammie. Especially when Peyton had opted to stay in Oregon to help Drew with his sports medicine practice. Did Thomas Wright doubt that Grit and Grace would succeed? Did he believe a bunch of women, former reality TV stars—using the term loosely—had no chance competing against very successful men?

A very real possibility if they couldn't get their potential investors to stop talking to each other long enough to watch Emma ride.

Then Sammie would have let these women get close for nothing. Just to be a part of something. The slow burn that had taken up residency behind Sammie's breastbone flared.

Before her mind could travel farther down that path, Emma popped up and began climbing the stairs to the platform above the bucking chute added to the metal pole corral-turned training arena. Sammie followed. Laura and Meira were already up there, readying the bronc they'd chosen for the demonstration while Beth waited in the arena to pull the gate.

The ranch manager, Justin Chadwick, who had been

hired by Peyton's brother and had come with the A Bar H, was acting as their pickup man—the cowboy tasked with helping the rider off the bronc after the buzzer sounded or running down the bronc if the rider was bucked off—and waited on the far side of the corral atop his big black gelding.

Emma turned to look back at Sammie. "Are you sure you don't want to be the one to ride Willie Bite?"

"Positive." Sammie made a show of putting her hand to the small of her back as she climbed the stairs. "I must have tweaked my back hoisting a bale of hay earlier."

Emma stopped in her tracks, concern radiating from her pale-blue eyes. "How bad?"

Guilt swamped Sammie. But there was nothing to be done about the need for subterfuge. At least not yet. Not until she'd come to grips with her new reality.

She mustered a reassuring smile for Emma, strengthened by the very real love she felt for her friends. "Not bad at all. Really. I promise."

Emma searched her face for a heart-stopping moment, lasting long enough to make Sammie want to tug down the brim of her cowboy hat.

Then Emma shrugged. "If you're sure. Promise you'll lay off buckin' bales for a few days."

"I promise."

"Good. And I'll try to remember to do that hair flick thing you always do if Willie decides to be lazy today. It's crazy how flipping your hair around makes a ride more impressive."

Sammie released the breath she'd been holding at having escaped Emma's scrutiny with a laugh. "That big chonk of a bronc won't let us down today. He's born to buck," Sammie said with a confidence in the bronc she didn't feel. Peyton's seed money had gone a long way toward setting up the Grit and Grace operation, but they needed investors if they were to survive for the long haul. Investors and rodeo contracts.

When Emma and Sammie reached the chute, Meira straightened from where she'd been checking Willie's flank strap. She gestured toward the men. "Look at them. Clumped together like a bunch of hens. And they call women gossipy."

Laura snorted. "One of them is even texting."

"Or probably googling us," Meira groused.

"With another one looking on," Emma added.

"They might not even be thinking about us." Sammie dropped her voice several octaves to imitate the man leaning to see the other man's phone. "Hey Carl, add this to your contacts. For a good time call 1-800-RIDE-MY-BULL."

The women erupted in a burst of laughter.

Sammie quickly shushed them. "Don't giggle. Do. Not. Giggle. We don't want to risk them saying that this"—she pointed at the G & G embroidered on the breast pocket of the white, button-down, long-sleeve shirt they all wore—"stands for Giggling Girls."

Nodding, Laura said, "We need them to take us seriously."

Meira planted her hands on her hips as she glared at the men from beneath her brown, wide-brimmed hat. "We need them to at least watch."

Emma climbed into the chute and said, "I'll make them watch."

She lowered herself onto the big roan saddle bronc, who snorted in protest. Or more likely, in warning. Willie Bite was Grit and Grace's newest and best bucker.

As quickly as she could, Emma slid her boots into the stirrups, took the thick, braided bronc rein from Meira, and firmly gripped the saddle horn with her free hand. Not wasting any time, she pushed her feet forward to settle her blunted spur rowels against Willie's shoulders, leaned as far back in the saddle as she could, and nodded.

Beth, standing in the corral, pulled the chute gate open and Willie Bite erupted outward. As usual, he leapt straight upward, propelling his huge, draft horse body ridiculously high.

At the peak of his jump, Emma let out the loudest "Woo-hoo" Sammie had ever heard.

Sure enough, the men all turned to watch. When Willie landed hard on four stiff legs only to instantly launch himself into a series of twisting and violent bucks, the men's attention was assured.

Well before eight seconds had passed, Emma made a big show out of being bucked off, complete with an extravagant flip of her long, platinum-blonde hair. She kicked free of the stirrups and allowed herself to be flung away from the bronc, landing hard in the deep, loose dirt. Today was about the animals' prowess, not the women's abilities in the arena.

Justin quickly maneuvered his horse between the bronc's flying hooves and Emma. Beth opened the exit chute gate and gave a whistle. Willie kicked impressively a few more times, then trotted out of the corral. The gelding was such a showoff.

Emma popped up, uninjured, but Sammie and the other women only had eyes for the men on the other side of the corral fence. There was an agonizing moment of silence, then they started to clap. Slowly at first, then raucously.

The warmth of triumph pushed aside the icy fear and uncertainty that had become a constant for Sammie from the moment Buckin' TV had cut them loose.

Since a single night had upended her plans for the future. She finally relaxed.

Right up until she noticed the tall cowboy dressed in pressed dark-washed jeans, a crisp, white button-down shirt and clapping and whistling the loudest. She froze in recognition.

Alec Neisson, the man who'd changed her life, was here.

SAMANTHA ABEL, THE only woman to have ever ghosted

Alec, had finally noticed him. He knew the second she'd spotted him by the way her tall, lithe body had stiffened and stilled. How, beneath her tan, wide-brimmed hat, her long, silky, dark-blonde hair, meticulously shaped into loose curls, blew unhindered across her beautiful face.

Clearly, she hadn't expected him to track her down. Not that he had. Not at all. He was simply taking a much-needed break and checking out the competition for his grandfather. Just seeing with his own eyes the environment the Wright Ranch rough stock his older brother Drew had asked for, would be living in.

True or not, that's what he would tell her. So what if he'd been more than a little surprised to wake up alone in the fifth wheel he used even when riding in his hometown rodeo? So what if she hadn't answered his calls or texts? So what if he hadn't been able to stop thinking of her? Though they'd flirted for days, they'd only spent the one night together. A hell of a night, but still . . .

When his grandfather had told him that the former Buckin' Babes, now owners of Grit and Grace Rodeo Roughstock Company, had put out an open invitation for potential investors to come check out their operations and that he wanted someone from the Wright Ranch to go, Alec had volunteered. No way could he pass up the chance to see Sammie again. Plus, the injury to his shoulder was a potent reminder that it was time to start planning for his future, and the future Alec wanted required proving himself to his grandfather.

The A Bar H Ranch itself, with its large, renovated main house, constructed entirely from amber, tan, and rusty-brown stone and heavy, dark timber and impeccable barns and outbuildings, rivaled his own family's ranch in Central Oregon. The A Bar H was larger than the Wright Ranch in terms of acreage. But everything was bigger in Texas, right? The former Buckin' Babes had scored a win when they leased this place.

Tuning out the typical sexist remarks being made by the regional-rodeo-big-money-good-old-boys, Alec settled his forearms on a corral rail and patiently watched from beneath the brim of his cowboy hat the woman he couldn't get out of his head.

The other women, beautiful and fit, with long hair in nearly every shade that would appear in the average male's fantasies, made their way toward the potential investors. Sammie hung back, her gaze shifting nervously between him and the others. Had he inadvertently done something so bad that she didn't want to be near him, let alone talk to him?

No. No way could he have misread the situation that badly. Misread her so completely. He had never laughed so hard, or loved so hard, with a woman. They had clicked in all the right ways. In all the right places.

The mere thought of the way their places clicked together had him reaching for the collar of his shirt as his temperature rose in a way that had nothing to do with the growing heat of the Texas sun. The way she'd thrown her head back and laughed unabashedly, how her bluebell-colored eyes had flared with passion, the way her satiny blonde hair had slipped between his fingers—More than enough fuel to get him hot under the collar.

It took one of the other women, a sun-kissed brunette—Laura, maybe, who'd asked so many questions about financial outlay when he'd given the Buckin' Babes a tour of the Wright Ranch when they'd been in Pineville—looking back toward Sammie and gesturing for her to join the group for Sammie to start moving. She visibly gathered herself, squaring her shoulders before striding forward. She was nothing if not brave.

So why in the hell was she avoiding him?

Never one to back down from something, even if it was guaranteed to hurt, Alec pushed away from the metal corral railing and joined the party.

Sammie made her way to the front and spread her hands to gain the men's attention. "Welcome, gentlemen, to the Grit and Grace Rodeo Roughstock Company. My name is Sammie Abel. I'm in charge of marketing and procuring contracts for Grit and Grace. You just had the pleasure of watching Emma Barrett attempt to ride Willie Bite." Sammie gestured to Emma, who touched a finger to the brim of her cowboy hat and executed a cheeky curtsy.

The men clapped in appreciation.

Sammie continued, "We are lucky enough to have acquired Willie Bite's half-sibling, Betty Won't, who was also born to buck. As are the other broncs we have so far. Any investment you make with us here at Grit and Grace will gain you partial ownership of these magnificent animals. Invest enough and we will grant named ownership. Shared with us, of course."

Of course, Alec thought. He wondered what sort of deal his grandfather had agreed to when his brother Drew had asked him to help Drew's new fiancée's friends start their own rodeo roughstock company in Texas. Alec personally didn't care, but Thomas Wright didn't do anything without a reason. And if that reason gave Alec an excuse to be here long enough to find out what was going on with Sammie, then he was okay with it.

"If you'll follow us, we'll give you a tour of our bronc barn," Sammie said.

"What about bulls?" a short, stout man in a tan suit and white cowboy hat asked. "Do you have any bulls?"

Sammie answered, "We do. This ranch is home to some quality longhorn-and-Brahman mixed bloodlines that Meira Ware, our very own geneticist, believes have tremendous potential."

The mahogany-haired beauty—obviously Meira—nodded in agreement.

There were a few murmurs at the mention of a geneticist being amongst the sparkly jean-wearing hotties. These guys had no clue.

"But are any of you girls feisty enough to ride one of your bulls for us?" another man Alec recognized asked.

Alec could tell from the way the women stiffened that they didn't appreciate having their strength and bravery reduced to being "feisty." Let alone being called girls. He didn't appreciate it much, either.

Stepping forward, Alec said, "Now Mr. Meyer, you know as well as I do that only dumbasses like me are silly enough to climb aboard a longhorn-Brahman mix."

"Alec Neisson! That *is* you." Mr. Meyer extended his hand for Alec to shake. "What brings you here?"

"Much the same as you." That got their attention.

"Your grandfather is investing?"

Alec shrugged. "Thomas Wright is a smart man."

More murmuring and pointed looks between the men.

Grining, Alec met Sammie's gaze.

She was not smiling. Just the opposite.

He sobered. Clearly, he was stepping on her marketing toes.

The first guy to ask about bulls said, "Alec, are you willing to ride one of the bulls here? Just because a bull is a longhorn-and-Brahman mix doesn't automatically make him rank. I personally own one who is the biggest and laziest S.O.B. you'll ever see."

Alec didn't glance back at Sammie, but he could feel her stare, pointed and intense, as well as that of the other women. He might be a dumbass, but he was smart enough not to steal their thunder.

"Sorry, gentlemen." Alec made a show of rotating his right shoulder with an exaggerated grimace. "But I have to give this dislocated shoulder at least a couple more days' rest. It's why I was free to come on down here and spend some time on this amazing spread with these amazing ladies." Now he did look directly at Sammie again.

Her blue gaze was stormy.

He needed to get to the bottom of whatever was eating at her.

Mr. Meyer huffed. "So, no bull riding exhibition?"

Alec gave the older man his best *aw shucks* smile. "I'm awfully sorry, sir. Not today."

Sammie extended a hand toward the barns. "But what we do have available today is a tour of our facilities and an up-close look at the rough stock currently at Grit and Grace. If you'll follow Beth—"

Mr. Meyer interrupted. "Have you secured any contracts yet?"

The other women gave telling glances at each other, but Sammie's gaze remained steady. "As a matter of fact, I will be meeting with the Last Stand Rodeo committee soon." Then she smiled the smile Alec had come to think of as her show smile. "Now, how about that tour?"

The men finally started forward, with the women subtly herding them toward the barns as if they were distracted sheep.

Alec quickly skirted around them until he reached Sammie, touching a hand to her hip to get her attention. She glanced toward him, then stopped abruptly.

She frowned. "What are you doing here—"

Alec cut her off with a slight squeeze of his hand and a meaningful glance at the others moving past them, their curiosity clear.

At a pointed look from the platinum blonde named Emma, Sammie said, "I'll be right there," and shooed her away with her pasted-on smile.

Sammie waited until the group was well past them before turning to him. "Alec! Seriously, what are you doing here?" she hissed.

"Why haven't you answered my calls or texts?"

"Stalker much?"

"Come on, Sammie. You didn't even say goodbye. Did I do something?"

"No. Well, yes. I mean, *we* did something."

The very clear memory of all the things they'd done together that night raised his temperature faster than the Texas summer sun on pavement. "Damn straight we did something. We did a lot of something."

She shifted away from him, looking everywhere but at him. "That's not what I mean. But it is why I didn't say goodbye. I never expected spending a night with you to be so . . . so . . ."

"Good?"

She met his gaze. "Yes."

Alec softened his tone. "So you freaked out and ghosted me."

"Yes. I'm sorry. I freaked out a little and just left. But now . . . I have been meaning to call you. Really."

"Because?"

The blue of her eyes swam beneath the sheen of tears. "Because I'm pregnant, Alec."

Chapter Two

As Sammie fought the threatening tears, she watched the play of emotions on Alec's handsome face. Shock—maybe even horror—fought with disbelief and denial.

Panic and fear were threatening to consume her.

What had she done?

Her plan had been to keep her pregnancy a secret. At least until she'd secured the first rodeo stock contract for Grit and Grace from the local rodeo. Instead, she might have very well just screwed everything up by opening her big mouth and telling her secret to the one person with the most power over her.

While she didn't really believe he would be that vindictive, Alec had the power to affect her and her friends' future by telling his grandfather not to send the bulls and broncs Drew had arranged for them. And if Alec really wanted to, he could take over her life because she carried his child. Then he could use the wealth and power of his family to take the baby from her.

She had no wealth or power. She had no family. At least

none who would defend and support her. She had her friends, who were now also her partners, but she would never put them in the position of having to go against a powerhouse like the Wright Ranch.

What had she just done?

She'd told him her secret, that's what she'd done, because he had the right to know.

Sammie had never known her father, and she'd often wondered if he'd even known about her. Especially after her mom had dumped Sammie with her own mom and taken off. But her mother had been a teenager and, presumably, her father had been one, also, when they'd conceived Sammie, so any scenario was possible. Particularly when Sammie's grandmother had preached the best way to nab a man was to get knocked up, a tactic she espoused despite it not working for her or her daughter.

Sammie had sworn she would never go down that road. Yet here she was. And, unintentional or not, now Alec knew.

She had to convince him to keep the news of her pregnancy just between them. At least for a little while.

She watched Alec continue to battle his own emotions, the fight clear on his face. She couldn't tell which one was coming out on top until he met her gaze.

"How?"

Disbelief and denial for the win. Sarcasm was her personal go-to. Especially after things she'd never intended to say somehow managed to pop out of her mouth.

"And here I was believing that, based on your performance on our one and only night together, you knew exactly how the whole *Tab A into Slot B* thing worked."

"We used protection."

"We did." She gave him an expansive shrug, despite the tightness gripping her shoulders. "But unlike death and taxes..."

Alec ran a hand over his face, knocking his cowboy hat askew. "Nothing is guaranteed."

Dang it, he was so cute. Sammie softened her tone. "Not one hundred percent. Obviously."

Alec looked toward the horizon for a moment, then straightened his hat and hitched up his big boy britches. "And you're sure it's mine?"

Anger, hot and intense, washed away the admiration, and beneath that, the panic and fear. Sammie turned on her heel to leave him in the Texas dust. She might talk a big game, claiming to be a master at lovin' 'em and leavin' 'em, but she'd really thought Alec had seen through her smoke and mirrors. Which was exactly why she'd ghosted him in the first place. He'd scared her, plain and simple. A man like him would be too easy to fall for. But she wouldn't have him questioning her on this.

"Sammie! Wait. Just wait."

She paused, fisting her hands at her sides and breathing deep to get a grip. After all, she needed him to agree to keep this secret. At least until she had the chance to prove herself.

The last thing she wanted was for anyone to cut her slack or give her opportunities because they pitied her.

She felt Alec's light touch on her waist through the substantial cotton of her button-down Grit and Grace logo shirt. His touch was as hot as she remembered. His voice was soft and thick with emotion as he spoke next to her ear. "I'm sorry. Okay? I'm sorry."

The heat of his touch melted her anger as effectively as his gentle apology. This guy really got to her. She'd have to be careful. So very, very careful. She couldn't risk the success of Grit and Grace because she was distracted by some cowboy.

She turned slowly to face him. "I would never... If I wasn't sure, Alec, I would never—"

He tightened his hold on her waist and raised his other hand to cup her cheek. His palm was rough with well-earned calluses, but his touch on her face was incredibly gentle. "I know," he whispered, his voice as rough as his callused hands and no less compelling. "I know, Sammie. You just really caught me off guard. I need a second to wrap my head around this."

She was gripped by the urge to nuzzle his palm. She stepped back away from him instead.

He let her go, but kept his hands raised as if he were trying to settle a skittish horse.

She said, "You can have as much time as you need. As long as you keep this"—she pointed at her still flat belly—

"to yourself."

His blond brows went up. "You haven't told..." He gestured in the direction of the bronc barn where her friends were taking the potential investors.

She vehemently shook her head. "No. No, no, no. *No.* Not yet. I don't want anyone to know until I've had a chance to land the contract to provide the rough stock for the Last Stand Rodeo."

Alec lowered his hands. "You don't have to prove yourself to anyone, Sammie."

This guy... Sammie dropped her head back, searching the already hazy blue sky for inspiration on how to hold at bay the only man with the ability to read her so quickly and accurately.

"You're—what, five weeks?"

Sammie pulled in a steadying breath and looked at Alec again. "Yes."

"That's not very far along. When did you find out?" Alec asked in a near whisper.

"For sure? Three days ago."

His expressive blue eyes narrowed. "You okay?"

Her heart gave a little bump. "Yes. So far. But like you said, I'm not very far along."

"Good. Good." His gaze dropped to her stomach—or, more accurately, her occupied womb—then drifted to the corral. "I wondered why Emma had ridden Willie Bite and not you. That was smart."

"It happens occasionally."

The corner of his mouth lifted just a little, but he kept his gaze on the corral. She could tell his brain was working fast and furiously. A familiar dread settled heavily in Sammie's gut.

She lowered her chin. "Promise me you won't tell anyone yet."

"Marry me."

"*What?*"

"Marry me, Sammie. You know I was raised to do the right thing—"

"Just stop. Stop right now." Sammie shut Alec down with the same force that she brought a mental heel down on the part of her screaming *yes, yes, yes* to his incredibly lame proposal. "I am not marrying you, Alec."

Too late, Sammie thought to look around and make sure none of her partners or ranch hands or, god forbid, potential investors were near. Blessedly, she and Alec were still alone in the space between the corral and the barns. She pulled in a steadying breath. "I didn't get knocked up to trap myself a big-name pro bull rider, even when that big name happens to be Alec Neisson of the Wright Ranch."

She could tell by the look on his face the thought had crossed his mind, however briefly. The knowledge that he might not trust her hit her like a hoof to the chest. But getting on him for not trusting would be a clear case of the pot calling the kettle black. She'd sprout wings and fly before she trusted anyone out of hand.

There was no way in hell she would marry him because she was pregnant. She refused to give her grandmother that win by proving her right. If she married, and it was a big if, she would do it because she'd found a man who wanted to be with her. Because of what she was on the inside, not because she was pretty or pregnant.

And there was no way she would risk her heart for the likes of Alec Neisson, with the money, close-knit family, and power to take her child and leave her with nothing.

"I NEED TO hear you say that you promise not to tell anyone, Alec. If you say that you promise, then I know you won't tell."

Alec was still too stunned to do anything but comply. "I promise I won't tell." But he refused to pretend as if nothing had happened between them.

The tension visibly left her, and her shoulders dropped. "Thank you."

"For now. But obviously we can't keep the pregnancy secret forever. And I refuse to pretend as if I'm not the one responsible."

"You're not the only one responsible, Alec. I was there, too, you know. It takes two—"

He held up a hand to stop her. "I know. You're right.

I'm sorry."

Alec readjusted his hat. Sammie telling him she was pregnant with his child was the very last thing he'd expected when he'd come to the A Bar H. He'd been looking for answers for why she'd ghosted him. She'd said she'd ghosted him because she'd been freaked out by how good they were together. The exact opposite of what he'd feared. He'd thought for sure that he'd screwed up somehow, that he'd said the wrong thing, done the wrong thing. But she hadn't wanted him because he'd done everything right? What the hell?

One thing he knew for sure, he was going to be a part of his child's—and his child's mother's—life.

He met her beautiful blue gaze and did his best to infuse steel into his own. "I need a promise from you, too, Samantha."

She slow-blinked at his use of her formal name. "Which is?"

He could tell from her hard tone she was gearing up for battle. Well, buckle up, babe. "I need you to promise me that you will let me be a part of this journey with you."

"Alec, I can't—"

"Yes, you can, Sammie. Because, as you said, it took two of us to make this baby. And I believe in my soul that it takes two—or more—people to raise a child."

Sammie made a rude noise and rolled her eyes. "Of course you do. Considering your family—"

"My childhood wasn't exactly all BBQs and pony rides. Don't make assumptions, Sammie."

She let out a frustrated breath and stepped forward, placing a hand on his chest. "I'm sorry. You're right. What I said came out wrong." She dropped her gaze to his boots, but her fingers flexed slightly on his pec, triggering some very vivid memories.

"What I meant..." She raised her gaze to his, and the pain he saw made him quickly place his own hand over hers, trapping it against his heart. "I meant to say that you've always known you were wanted. That you were loved. I didn't have that growing up. Not even close. My grandmother—"

"Not your mom?" The old, deep wound pulsed in a familiar way.

"See, this is part of the problem. We knew each other well, biblically—"

"Really well."

The appreciation, the warmth he infused in his tone, brought her up short for a beat. He watched her shake it off. "Yes. Really well. But we didn't get to know each other... not biblically."

"We would have if you hadn't ghosted me."

She pulled her hand from beneath his and stepped away from him. "You're right. You're one hundred percent right. That's on me. But the fact remains, we don't really know each other."

"Easy enough to solve. I'm here now. You're here. Let's get to know each other. I'll help you with whatever you need, and you can concentrate on growing our baby."

Sammie's face went white at the mention of *their baby*. "I don't need your help, Alec."

He threw up his hands in frustration. "I know you don't need my help. But I'm offering it, anyway." He stepped forward and gripped her shoulders, trying to somehow convey the storm of emotions crashing through him. "I know you don't need me. I know you are strong and capable and . . . and stubborn. But I want you to. I want you to need me, Sammie. I want you to let me be a father to this child. Please."

Sammie's body was rigid beneath his hands, and he had a horrible moment of terror when he thought he may have gone too far, that maybe she would shut him completely out of both her and their child's life, but then she relaxed to the point she swayed toward him. It took everything in Alec not to pull her tight into his arms.

As if sensing what he was about to do, Sammie stiffened again and stepped out of his grip. "Okay, Alec. Of course. Of course, I'll let you be a part of our—" her voice caught. "Of our child's life. I know you'll be an amazing dad. But you need to let me live my own life. This baby and I are not a package deal for you. I'm going to live up to my part of Grit and Grace. I refuse to let my partners down. Do you understand what I'm saying?"

Alec buried his hands in his front pockets to keep from reaching for her again. "I understand, Sammie. Completely. But you're also not getting rid of me anytime soon. And I meant it when I said I want to help. In any way."

The noise of indistinct but boisterous chatter drew Alec and Sammie's attention as the group of potential investors and the other Grit and Grace partners emerged from the bronc barn.

Clearly grateful for the interruption, Sammie gave what he interpreted as a *we'll finish this later* wave and turned to trot toward the group.

Alec could only watch her go. She wouldn't be getting rid of him anytime soon because he knew, deep in his heart, that he couldn't trust her any farther than he could throw her.

But he was determined to be a father in every way to their child, whether Samantha Abel wanted him or not.

Chapter Three

"ARE ANY OF us *feisty* enough to ride a bull? Seriously?" Emma gestured wildly with the dangerously full pitcher of sweet tea she'd carried from the kitchen.

Sammie looked up from the dinner plate settings she was laying out on the huge, rough-hewn, ten-person dining room table in the beautifully remodeled main house of the A Bar H. Emma had been raging ever since the potential investors left.

Meira emerged from the large gourmet kitchen carrying the salad she'd become famous for with her fellow Buckin' Babes. "Get used to it, ladies. It'll take the local good ol' boys a while to accept what we're capable of." She set the large wooden bowl of salad precisely in the center of the table runner, then retreated into the kitchen.

Emma slammed the pitcher on the table with enough force to slosh it. "Feisty? They want feisty? I'll show them feisty."

Sammie saluted Emma with a designer stoneware plate that had come with the house. "Attagirl, Emma. No one is going to take us seriously until we prove ourselves."

Laura pulled up short, a basket of garlic bread in hand. "By riding *bulls?*"

"No." Sammie set the last plate down. "Unless you want to, that is. More power to you if you do."

"I'll pass, thanks," Laura said with a shudder and added the bread to the growing spread in the center of the table, then headed back to the kitchen. While Laura wouldn't blink at having to ride a huge draft horse crossbred with a devil, she was not a fan of the bulls, the literal cash cows of the rodeo roughstock game. Sammie didn't mind them, but there was no way she'd try to ride one. Even before she'd found herself *in the family way.* Beth, on the other hand, loved them and thought they were terribly misunderstood.

Sammie turned toward the sideboard where the silverware was kept and said, "It's not a matter of actually riding the bulls, but rather making those men, and all the people like them, believe we can. If we wanted to."

"Which we don't!" Laura yelled from the kitchen.

"We don't have to, is my point. But we make them think we can." Sammie retrieved the cutlery from its drawer and began completing the place settings.

Emma glowered and took a seat. "Easy for you to say. You can convince a fly to pass by a turd."

Or convince a family-first cowboy to keep secret the existence of his unborn child. At least, Sammie prayed she had convinced Alec. What if she hadn't?

Suddenly weak in the knees, Sammie quickly finished setting the table and sank into the chair she'd made a habit of sitting in during their communal meals.

What if she hadn't convinced Alec to keep her—their—secret? What if he'd simply said what she'd wanted to hear, and was at this very moment sitting in his room at the Bluebonnet Inn, or wherever he was staying, calling home with the news there was a new member of the Neisson clan on the way?

Sammie's stomach roiled ominously. When Meira returned to the dining room, carrying a bowl of pasta, followed by Laura with the very aromatic marinara sauce, Sammie made a grab for her water glass and took a series of small sips to keep from being sick.

Oh no. Not already. She hadn't thought she'd be hit by morning sickness—which should be called the all-day barfies—until she was farther along. But what did she know of pregnancy? Nothing. Absolutely nothing. She needed to find an obstetrician in Last Stand.

Maybe this awful feeling wasn't morning sickness. Maybe the mouthwatering—not in a good way—nausea had been caused by the fact that her life was steadily spiraling out of her control.

No. This awful feeling wasn't caused by a lack of control. Sammie knew the sinking dread of having no agency in life. She had experienced that leaden sensation virtually every morning upon waking right up until she'd left her grandmother's house for good. Joining the women's ranch bronc circuit, and subsequently the *Buckin' Babes* television show, had been both liberating and settling. What she was feeling now was an entirely different sort of unsettled.

As the other women took their seats around the table and began passing the pitcher of iced sweet tea, Sammie carefully breathed through her mouth to avoid what she would have normally considered wonderful aromas.

Laura raised her glass of tea. "Male attitudes aside, here's to our first, and hopefully, fruitful, demonstration and tour. Cheers, ladies."

There was a chorus of *cheers* and raised glasses.

Sammie, having passed on the sweet tea, clinked her water glass against her friends' glasses.

Beth caught her eye when their glasses touched. "Kinda wild that Alec Neisson, the precious baby and pro bull rider from the Wright Ranch, showed up for our very first demo." The hitch of her raven eyebrows made her meaning clear to Sammie. She believed Alec had followed Sammie here.

Sammie froze.

Emma said slyly, "Pretty sure he didn't come for the demo. We all saw how he and our Sammie-girl danced together the night we were fired."

"You mean the night we took control of our lives," Beth corrected.

Meira nodded. "True that. But as far as Alec Neisson showing up here... I don't think it's all that wild," she mused. "It makes sense for Thomas Wright to send him to check out our ranch ahead of sending the stock Drew gave us. Especially since Alec can't ride bulls in competition until his shoulder heals." Leave it to Meira to seek out a logical explanation.

Relief at having an excuse to latch on to flooded Sammie. She quickly nodded and pointed at Meira as if she'd hit the nail on the head.

If only Meira's supposition were true.

A voice in Sammie's head cried foul. That she didn't really wish the only reason Alec appeared on their leased Texas ranch was to make sure the Wright Ranch bulls and broncs received exemplary room and board. But, in her heart of hearts, did she really wish that the only reason Alec showed up on the A Bar H was in pursuit of her?

Maybe. If it were just her now.

But it wasn't. It wasn't just her occupying this space anymore. A part of Alec lived beneath her heart. Combined with a part of her. She couldn't claim to hate that reality. Because she didn't. Her heart ached from how much she didn't hate it. But she did hate the threat to her plans. To her independence. To everything she'd worked so hard to escape.

For the millionth time she heard her grandmother's voice in her head saying *Samantha, the best way to snag a guy is to have an oops*—her grandmother's wholly inappropriate term for trapping a man with an unplanned pregnancy.

And it had worked, hadn't it? Alec, of the multimillion-dollar Wright Ranch dynasty, had asked Sammie to marry him. Because, and only because, she'd told him she was pregnant with his child.

For that reason alone, she could never marry him.

The bowl of noodles was thrust beneath her nose.

"Sammie, spaghetti?" Emma asked in a way that made Sammie believe it wasn't the first time Emma had asked the question.

"Oh! Yes. Sorry." She took the thankfully aromatically benign bowl from Emma. She should be able to handle plain noodles.

Sammie had barely scooped a moderate helping of pasta onto her plate before she found the bowl of accompanying marinara sauce being passed to her.

The wave of oregano and garlic smell hit her so hard she almost hurled. How would she ever keep this pregnancy a secret at least a little longer if she was going to be hit by all-day morning sickness so soon? But she was resolved not to tell anyone—other than Alec, who she'd really hoped to tell later—until she'd secured their first contract.

Only then would she have proven herself capable of being more than just the vessel for procreation her grandmother had declared her to be. Not to mention, prove to the men who would so quickly dismiss them that she and her friends were more than capable of doing the job of raising rank rodeo rough stock and, more importantly, doing it well.

Sammie could feel Emma's gaze intent on her, so she took the bowl of sauce that Sammie would have normally happily gorged herself on and pretended as if it didn't contain something vile. She made a show of scooping a large spoonful of the sauce but smeared only a tiny amount onto the pasta she hoped to be able to eat. She nearly shoved the bowl of marinara at Beth seated directly across from her, then snatched the bread from Emma. All she'd need to do was surreptitiously remove the part of the bread slathered with garlic butter, and she'd be good to go.

Beth finished ladling a hearty serving of sauce onto her pasta, then scrutinized Sammie. "So . . . what did he say?"

"He who?" Sammie desperately aimed for nonchalance as she tore off a chunk of bread crust and popped it into her mouth.

Beth rolled her eyes. "The Neisson hottie, who else? You talked to him for some time while we were showing the other guys around. Is Alec going to endorse our setup to his grandfather? Or do we need to start looking elsewhere for the rest of the bulls and broncs we need?"

"Um . . . He didn't exactly say," Sammie hedged.

Meira groaned. "We're screwed if we don't get those animals from the Wright Ranch. I honestly doubt we'll land the funding we need without that caliber of bloodstock."

Sammie rushed to reassure her. "I don't think we need to worry about that just yet. I mean, once I secure our first rodeo contract, the investors will commit to funding us. I just know they will."

Laura sighed and set her fork down. "But how will we land a contract without the stock?"

Sammie felt herself deflating. "With charm and good manners?"

Emma laughed, just as she was putting a fork full of heavily sauced spaghetti in her mouth, and sprayed marinara all over the place, sending everyone into a fit of very messy laughter.

Laura shook her head. "We are so screwed."

Meira wiped her mouth. "No, we're not. Have faith." She sent Sammie a meaning-laden look. "I do."

Sammie could only smile back with as much bravado, however false, she could muster.

Deep down, though, Sammie was terrified. What if she didn't have what it took to convince the local rodeo officials to take a chance on a brand-new, women-owned-and-run rodeo roughstock company? What if she didn't have what it took to be a good mother, considering the poor examples her own mother and grandmother had provided her? What if Alec decided this baby would be better served away from her, in a world of luxury and influence provided by the Neissons and their patriarch, Thomas Wright?

She looked around her at the very comparable luxury she and her friends had lucked into finding themselves living in, all thanks to Peyton Halliday's sway over her oldest brother.

This ranch was incredible. But like seemingly everything in Sammie's life right now, their stay here on this ranch was dependent on Sammie securing their first contract.

She couldn't fail.

And she couldn't let Alec Neisson distract her.

"I WANTED TO make sure you don't mind," Alec said into his cell phone and leaned back in the lone armchair in his room at Last Stand's Bluebonnet Inn. He'd wracked his brain, and this was the best plan—pretty much the only plan—he'd been able to come up with.

"Whether I mind or not isn't the issue," Asher Halliday said, his deep voice resonating in the way of men used to being in charge. "Those ladies have a valid one-year lease, you know. It's their call."

"I'm aware." And was precisely why Alec had called Asher. Alec was determined to be there for Sammie, for their child, whether she wanted him or not. A determination that bordered on desperation, thanks to Sammie's insistence to keep the pregnancy secret.

Alec leaned forward in the chair and settled an elbow on his knee. "I thought it might be easier to convince them to let me stay on the ranch and help out as much as I can while my shoulder heals if I have your blessing."

"Any particular reason you want to be there?"

"Yeah, one. Named Samantha."

"Ah. Understood." Asher was silent for a moment, obviously thinking. "There is a clause in the lease that allows me to retain control of the employees I'd hired to work the A Bar H after the renovations were complete. We could say you are working for me."

"Sounds good, boss," Alec quipped, despite the growing sense of guilt creeping up his throat. He knew it was underhanded to go to his brother's future brother-in-law, a man Alec had met only once at an engagement party thrown by the Hallidays, but Alec didn't exactly have a choice. He needed to be there for his child.

"As long as you clear it with Justin Chadwick, my ranch manager, who you'd be sharing the bunkhouse with. I have zero problems with you staying at the A Bar H while you recoup. I mean, come on, we're almost family." Asher Halliday laughed ruefully. "I still can't believe my baby sister is going to be married. To a doctor, no less. She always hated doctors."

"Drew is a good guy. You've got nothing to worry about." As much as Alec loved his other siblings, he had always had a deeper relationship with Drew. Mostly because they were close in age, but they also seemed to understand each other more.

"I know. Hard habit to break."

"There are far worse habits." Namely Alec's penchant for a certain lanky blonde bronc rider who wanted nothing to do with him.

"Indeed. Good luck, Alec. Feel free to call me if you need anything else."

Alec thanked and said goodbye to the other man, who reminded him more than a little of Alec's own oldest brother, Ian. Men with strong principles and even stronger will.

Alec had his own principles, which was why he wouldn't break his promise to Sammie and would keep her pregnancy secret. But his will was more than strong enough to not let her shut him out.

THE NEXT MORNING Alec had already spoken with Justin, the ranch manager, and was unloading his things from the truck he'd rented in Austin and had parked in front of the bunkhouse when the women of Grit and Grace started making their way down from the main house.

Unlike yesterday, when they'd been dressed in somewhat subdued, but no less eye-catching, rodeo spangles with their long, shiny hair down and curled, today, they were dressed for everyday ranch work. But even in scuffed boots, saddle-worn jeans, faded T-shirts or flannel, and with ponytails swinging beneath sweat-stained cowboy hats, these women were still flowers in a desert. The tallest of the women in particular. Sammie was mesmerizing. Talking to dark-haired Beth, Sammie moved with an easy, athletic grace.

She took his breath away.

Emma, the platinum-blonde firecracker, called, "Alec! You're back."

Sammie stopped dead, her gaze searching until it landed on him. With the other women continuing to walk toward him, he could see her forcing herself to move as well.

Alec pulled off his hat, holding it over his surprisingly pounding heart. "I am. I sincerely hope you all don't mind."

Laura chided, "You're in Texas now, Neisson. It's *y'all.*"

"My mistake, y'all." Alec bowed with no small amount of cheek.

Sammie drew close enough to sharply ask, "What are you doing here?"

Bright with hope, Meira asked, "Are the Wright Ranch stock coming?"

Alec had no idea. "Soon." He would call Ian to find out ASAP. If he called his grandpa directly, who knew what he'd blurt out? Thomas Wright had an uncanny way of getting the truth out of people. Especially his grandchildren. Until Sammie released Alec from his promise of secrecy, he'd be wise not to talk to Grandpa.

Beth asked, "How soon? Because if it's *soon* soon, I'll have to prep the stalls, make sure we have the proper feed—"

Alec held out his hat to slow her train. "I promise I'll give you a heads-up in plenty of time."

"Alec, what *are* you doing here?" Sammie repeated her question, her tone edging toward dark.

He returned his hat to his head like it was a helmet being donned for battle, then met her stormy blue eyes. "Asher Halliday, my soon-to-be sister-in-law's brother, hired me to be on hand to help out as needed. While my shoulder heals," he quickly added.

While it was true his shoulder would benefit from some time away from the pro bull riding circuit, he hadn't intended to take much time off. But plans change. Sometimes a lot.

Sammie frowned fiercely and opened her mouth to definitely protest, but Laura spoke first.

"Halliday *hired* you?"

Alec grinned. "Turns out he can afford me."

Laura threw up her hands. "All righty then." Clearly considering the matter closed, she continued to the nearest barn, where she could be heard yelling, "Yo, Justin! You good with Neisson working here?"

From somewhere in the barn, Justin called back, "Yep."

Beth hurried up to Alec. "How well do you know the bulls Drew arranged to send us? What can you tell me about them?"

He smiled reassuringly at her. "I promise an up-close meet and greet as soon as they get here."

"Thank you." Beth's smile was pure bliss before she followed after Laura.

Emma sidled up to him, and Alec went rigid with panic.

"Are any of your bull riding buddies coming to help too?" she asked.

Alec relaxed with the assurance her amorous interests weren't directed at him. "Sorry. Just me." When she deflated, he added, "For now."

That perked her up. "Cool. Well, I'll let you get to it." She turned toward the bronc stable, then tossed over her shoulder, "I'm sure Sammie will gladly help you get settled."

Alec glanced at Sammie and immediately knew the only place she'd gladly help him get settled in was a shallow grave.

She waited until they were alone by his truck before she said, "You're staying."

"I am."

"*Here.*"

He softened his tone. "Yes."

"Why?" The pain, the anguish, the fear in that one word spurred Alec into motion.

He closed the space between them and placed a gentle hand over their child. "You know why, Sammie. I want to help."

She stepped back, away from his touch. "I don't need your help."

"I know. I know you don't need anything from anyone. But that doesn't stop me from wanting to help you. I'm going to be here for you, Samantha. And our child."

"Shhh!" She whirled on her boot heel and, as she walked away from him, said, "What you are going to do is stay away from me, Alec. And don't call me Samantha."

Chapter Four

"YOU DO KNOW he earned his name, right?" Emma asked from the stall where she was brushing down the big chestnut named Betty Won't. Sammie was grooming Betty's half-brother, Willie Bite, in the neighboring stall.

Sammie paused the curry comb mid-stroke on Willie's withers, glancing quickly at the teeth end of the big gelding. Willie was giving her hard side-eye, so Sammie gentled the pressure she applied to the brush as she resumed running the stiff rubber bristles over Willie's coat, a reddish brown sprinkled with white. Seeming to approve of a less angry approach to grooming, Willie turned his attention to his wall-mounted hay feeder, yanking a mouthful of hay from between the galvanized steel bars.

Sammie looked across Willie's back and found Emma watching her as she absently brushed down Betty Won't.

"Is your back still bothering you?" Emma asked.

"What?" Then Sammie remembered the lie she'd told Emma yesterday to account for why she hadn't wanted to ride. "Oh. No. It's a lot better."

"Okay. Good." Emma paused for a couple of brush strokes, then added, "But it seems to me like something is bugging you."

Being bugged was one way to put how Sammie was feeling. She bent to check Willie's hoof to avoid responding to Emma's obvious fishing. While on the rodeo exhibition tour for the *Buckin' Babes* TV show, Sammie had only felt a real connection with Peyton Halliday. Once Sammie, Laura, Beth, Meira, and Emma had arrived in Texas and settled in at the A Bar H, though, they all had bonded in a way Sammie hadn't expected.

She and the other women were starting to know each other on a deeply personal level. Which meant the next few months were going to be that much harder to hide her pregnancy and the identity of the father. But Sammie wasn't ready to deal with her new reality yet.

She picked a small rock from the raised V, called the frog, that extended from the horse's heel into the underside of the hoof, smoothing her finger over the spot to check for tenderness. Despite spending most of her life wearing a mask of false bravado to hide her insecurities, Sammie feared she wouldn't be able to fool these smart and caring women for another day, let alone however many days it might take her to secure the Last Stand rodeo roughstock contract.

Satisfied Willie's hoof was fine, Sammie straightened and continued grooming him. She glided the brush over Willie's back and flank, following it with the palm of her free hand to smooth out his occasional twitches. To calm him. She needed to calm herself. Emma was right. If Sammie wasn't careful, Willie would react to her inattentive roughness with either his namesake bite or worse. Horses required a person to be present in the moment, not distracted by worries or fears. To focus on each individual task.

A focus that would be difficult for her with Alec not just in Last Stand, but right here on the A Bar H. He stirred up all the anger, panic, fear, and a sneaky dose of pleasure she'd been trying to get a handle on since she'd discovered she was pregnant. Heck, since the morning after she'd spent a night in his arms.

Though she'd told him to stay away from her, she had no doubt he'd do his best to be underfoot, to *help* her. Or, more likely, to manage her at best, control her at worst.

She couldn't let either happen. She'd worked too hard to make a life for herself. One that she loved. A life to be proud of. A life, she realized with shocking clarity, that she couldn't wait to share with her child.

So, it was up to her to avoid Alec if she wanted to keep hold of the reins of her life. And do her best to concentrate on finding ways to connect with the local rodeo officials.

"*Sammie.*"

Emma's entreaty pulled Sammie from her thoughts. She looked up and found Emma leaning on the chest-high wall separating Willie Bite and Betty Won't's stalls, her hands threaded through the bars that extended the barrier another two feet.

"I'm sorry, Emma. What did you say?"

"I asked, what are you going to do today? Maybe give a certain hunky bull rider a personal tour of the spread?"

Not likely. Sammie gave Willie a final pat and let herself out of his stall. "Actually, I'm going to call the Last Stand Rodeo's secretary and set up an appointment to make a pitch for next year's roughstock contract."

Emma hurried out of Betty's stall. "Do you really think they'll meet with you?"

"Absolutely."

Because she wouldn't take no for an answer.

THANKS TO HIS sister Caitlin, Alec knew when a woman told a man to stay away from her, he'd damn well better keep his distance. At least for the day.

He'd spend the day getting settled in the bunkhouse that more than rivaled the one at the Wright Ranch, even though his brother Ian, who managed their ranch, preferred to call it the employee housing. Ian had his own separate house on the Wright Ranch, but Justin Chadwick, the A Bar H's ranch manager, had to make do with this bunkhouse. Not that it was roughing it by any stretch of the imagination.

Asher Halliday had put his family's billions to good use when he'd overhauled the A Bar H Ranch. According to

Justin, Asher had drastically remodeled the bunkhouse, changing the large, dormitory-style space into single rooms off a main hallway. While the occupants still had to share a common bathroom and kitchen, it wasn't much of a hardship, considering everything was new and state-of-the-art. And there wasn't a bunk bed in sight. There was even a new hot tub right behind the bunkhouse, just for the hands, perfect for sore bones after a day in the saddle.

All in all, not a bad place to cool his heels.

Something he wasn't great at. Patience had never been a strong suit.

But one thing Alec had in spades was determination. Pretty much a job requirement for anyone who intended to make it as a professional bull rider. He was determined to be a part of his child's life. Sammie's baby would know him as "Dad." With the capital *D*. He wouldn't accept anything less. And if he could get Sammie to view him as someone she could trust, someone she could rely on regardless of the situation, all the better.

Alec pulled another pair of jeans from his duffle bag and placed them neatly in the middle drawer of the stylish, rough-hewn dresser that matched the queen bed dominating the room. Mounted on the wall directly opposite of the bed was a flat-screen TV. Definitely not a bad place at all to wait out a stubborn woman.

The alternative was to return to the grind of the pro bull riding circuit, messed-up shoulder or not, competing in everything everywhere until his body gave out for good.

No. This baby was his sign. It was time for him to start planning for his future.

A future that included his child. Which was nonnegotiable.

But there was also the matter of a certain blonde. The woman he couldn't get out of his head. Hell, she'd taken up permanent residence in his dreams. He'd wear her down, get her to trust him, and then they could decide how to proceed. First and foremost, as parents to their child.

He finished unpacking, then sat on the bed, which was covered by a thick burgundy comforter. While he didn't exactly rough it in the fifth wheel he traveled the circuit in, this place didn't suck.

Alec nodded to himself as resolve coursed through him. He would give Sammie the space she wanted, for a limited time, but no way in hell would he give up.

Too bad if she didn't like it.

SAMMIE JAMMED HER finger against the red dot on her cell phone screen, even though Regina Rhinehart, Last Stand Rodeo's secretary and all-around queen pooh-bah, had already disconnected the call from her end. Resisting the urge to chuck her phone across the dining room, Sammie settled for sliding it away from her in disgust. She pulled the ponytail band from her hair and scrubbed at her sore scalp.

"Bad news?" Laura asked from the kitchen doorway, wiping her hands on a dish towel. Normally, she spent the afternoons in the main house's office, staring at spreadsheets and trying to optimize their minimal funds.

Things must be dire if she was already in the kitchen.

Sammie was tempted to lie, to tell Laura the Last Stand rodeo officials couldn't wait to hear Sammie's pitch, that they were super excited to be the first rodeo to give the newly formed Grit and Grace Rodeo Roughstock Company a chance at winning their contract. But she felt guilty enough keeping her condition a secret. *Condition.* What a joke. As if pregnancy was like eczema or something.

"Sammie?"

"Sorry. I'm just losing my mind." She dropped her hands from her hair and turned to face Laura. "Only sort of bad news. I couldn't get a formal, scheduled-on-the-calendar kind of meeting with the local rodeo officials."

"But . . . ?"

"But Secretary Rhinehart did let slip that the rodeo officials tend to gather at the Last Stand Saloon on Tuesdays."

Laura raised a very skeptical tawny brow. "Let slip?"

Sammie sighed. "I tried to schedule a meeting on every day of the week. At any time. They were always busy. She was specific about their schedules."

Flipping the dish towel onto her shoulder, Laura closed the distance between them and placed a hand on Sammie's shoulder. "So go get 'em on Tuesday night."

"That's the plan. I'll need to get there, though. Do you know if anyone intends to use the ranch truck Tuesday?"

"Not as far as I know. Go ahead and take it. But when Meira and I drove it into town for groceries, it was low on gas. Make sure you fill up the tank before you leave."

"Will do."

"And remember, Sammie, if anyone can convince the Last Stand Rodeo officials that we're worth taking a chance on, it's you."

Sammie's throat grew tight. "Thank you, Laura."

She gave Sammie's shoulder an encouraging squeeze, then released her and turned back to the kitchen. "Thank me by helping to cut up this chicken. You know I hate to cook."

Sammie grinned and pushed away from the table. "If you hate it, then why are you so good at it?"

"Because I'm good at everything, darlin'," Laura called from the kitchen.

"Ain't we all?" Sammie shot back.

If only it were true.

"I'M ASSUMING YOU'RE familiar with longhorns?"

Alec shifted his forearms on the split-rail fence that enclosed the near pasture and looked at Justin, leaning on the same fence next to him. The older man, who was probably close to Alec's brother Liam in age, so mid-thirties, was squinting against the late afternoon sun as he surveyed the small herd of longhorn cattle grazing on the other side of the fence.

This bunch, with their impressive long, curved horns extending several feet, gleaming coats of brown, black, red, white, or a speckled combination of all those colors, and well-fed, but still athletic builds, had been separated from the larger herd and brought to this pasture. They were meant to serve as eye candy for the potential investors and rodeo officials, if any happened to stop by. Nothing like the very symbol of Texas, expertly cared for and clearly thriving, to instill confidence in a rodeo roughstock company.

"If 'by familiar with,' you mean I've stuck to one for eight seconds, then yes."

"I'm guessing you mean you're familiar with dehorned half-longhorn, half-something else."

Alec laughed. "Yes, sir. That is exactly what I mean."

The corner of Justin's mouth twitched upward as he gave a short nod. "I expect you'll learn quick enough."

"Wouldn't have survived four older siblings if I couldn't."

Again with the mouth twitch. Justin might be close to Liam in age, but he appeared to have embraced the stoic cowboy persona like Alec's oldest brother, Ian, had. Maybe managing a very high-end roughstock ranch did that to a man. Personally, Alec didn't need to run the whole show.

But the bull program on a very high-end roughstock ranch... that would be a dream come true.

Thinking of what Asher had told him the night before about having hired Justin himself, Alec asked, "How do you feel about Grit and Grace leasing the ranch?"

Justin eyed him from beneath the brim of his dusty brown cowboy hat. "You mean how do I feel about working for a bunch of women?"

Alec shrugged, not willing to characterize Sammie and her friends as *a bunch of women*.

"As long as they let me do my job the way it should be done, then I have no problem with them." He thought for a moment. "They are actual competitive bronc riders, after all."

In acknowledgement of the point of admiration, Alec said, "That they are."

Alec's cell phone buzzed and vibrated in his pocket. He pulled it out to check who was calling. When he saw the caller ID, he quickly said, "Will you excuse me? I have to take this."

"Go ahead," Justin said with a tilt of his head.

Alec walked away from the pasture fence toward the corral and, with ingrained-from-birth deference, pulled his hat from his head before he accepted the call. "Hey, Grandpa. How are you?"

"Alec. I'm just fine. How's the shoulder?"

Alec automatically rolled his shoulder, grimacing at the

bite of pain. "It's good. Giving it a rest has done wonders."

"I'm glad to hear it. The bull will always win if your shoulder doesn't stay in its socket."

True words. And all the more reason to get himself sorted. "Everything good at home?"

"Of course. I'm calling because I have a way to keep your rest time from being unproductive time."

That was Thomas Wright in a nutshell. If you're still breathing, you should be accomplishing something. "Oh?"

"I have a job for you while you're in Last Stand."

Alec's heart bumped. Hadn't he just been thinking about planning for his future? Proving himself to be of use to his grandfather was the all-important first step. "Whatever you need. Shoot."

"You're familiar with the local rodeo?"

"I've never competed in the Last Stand Rodeo, but I do know of it." Knew that Sammie and her friends were counting on next year's contract from that very rodeo to be the first rung on their ladder to success as rodeo roughstock contractors.

"Good. I've set up a meeting with their rodeo officials to negotiate a contract for the Wright Ranch to supply the stock for their next rodeo. I want you to be my representative and attend the meeting in my stead."

Alec took a step back, his grandfather's words hitting him with the force of a physical blow. "You want to bid for the Last Stand Rodeo contract?"

"Bid?" His grandfather's deep chuckle sounded like a rock being scraped against a cheese grater. "Our name is our bid. But details do need to be hammered out and paperwork submitted. I trust you to do that for me."

Heat infused Alec's chest. His grandpa trusted him. Wasn't that Alec's ultimate goal? Hadn't it always been? Securing the Last Stand Rodeo roughstock contract for the Wright Ranch would solidify that trust.

But at what cost?

He'd be hijacking the contract right out from underneath Grit and Grace.

Sammie, the mother of his unborn child, would never forgive him.

His grandfather proceeded to talk about the contract details Alec would need to negotiate, but Alec's mind wandered to what he considered more pressing details.

Claiming to be in the employ of Asher Halliday would keep him on the A Bar H, but Sammie would never let him close again. She was already avoiding him. If he took this contract away from her and her friends, he would never be able to stay close enough to keep an eye out for her, to help her. He'd never be able to prove himself worthy of being part of their child's life, before and after his—or her—birth. And he would certainly never be allowed to be a part of Sammie's life. The prospect hurt far more than her ghosting him had.

But he shouldn't forget that she *had* ghosted him. And she was adamant in not wanting him around now. She might never soften toward him. There was a very real chance he'd have to get the courts involved to be able to exercise his parental rights.

Did he give up everything he'd ever wanted, chasing after something that might never be?

He would be betraying Sammie by securing the Last Stand Rodeo roughstock contract for the Wright Ranch, but he would also prove himself capable to his grandfather. For his future.

Alec set his jaw and returned his hat to his head. As soon as his grandfather paused for a breath, Alec said, "I know what to do, Grandpa. When and where am I to meet with the Last Stand officials?"

"Tuesday, four p.m., at the Last Stand Saloon."

"You can count on me, Grandpa."

"Good. Don't let me down."

Chapter Five

TUESDAY EVENING AT a quarter to five, Sammie pulled the white pickup truck that had come with the ranch, bearing the A Bar H logo, into a newly vacated angled parking space right in front of the Last Stand Saloon on Main Street. She considered herself lucky to have snagged the parking spot. For a town of roughly ten thousand souls, Last Stand had what appeared to be a bustling downtown that had managed to hang on to its Old West charm.

On previous trips to town, she'd discovered that most of the businesses were on either Main or Hickory Street and were only a single block deep on either side of those roads. Definitely a small town, but Last Stand lacked for nothing, as far as Sammie could tell.

She put the truck in park, painfully aware of how sweaty her palms were on the gear shift and steering wheel. Never in her life had she been such a nervous, nauseous, scared, yet determined, jumbled mess. Not even when she'd climbed down into a chute and took her seat in the saddle of her very first rodeo bronc. She'd been scared then, yes, but she'd been in control. Now, not so much. The pregnancy hormones didn't help.

She really needed to calm down. For many reasons.

Because her and her child's future, and that of her friends, was riding on her ability to convince the local rodeo officials to give Grit and Grace a chance.

Flipping down the truck's visor, Sammie checked her pale-pink tinted lip gloss in the small mirror. According to the fan interaction generated by the *Buckin' Babes* reality TV show, the gloss had become her trademark. That and the long, loosely curled blonde tresses.

Sammie preferred to think of the lip gloss and styled long hair as armor. She could protect herself with nothing more than a distracting flick of her hair and purse of her lips. Keeping those who might hurt her at arm's length with a little superficial dazzle masquerading as perfection.

She needed to be perfect tonight. Her friends were depending on her. And while she was still struggling to wrap her brain around her pregnancy, her baby was depending on her. Sammie wanted to have secured their future by the time her little one arrived. There would be less risk of losing custody to the very wealthy, very connected Alec Neisson if she had her act together.

The awful thought propelled her out of the truck and onto the sidewalk, shielded from the hot Texas sun by the saloon's second-floor balcony, which was supported by evenly spaced and embellished posts. The rodeo secretary,

Regina Rhinehart, had said the men with the most immediate power to determine the success of Grit and Grace were meeting this evening at the saloon. Hopefully, Sammie would be able to figure out which of the patrons were the rodeo officials. Not an ideal way to start her quest for their first rodeo roughstock contract, but it was better than nothing.

Sammie hesitated, her nerves starting a thundering stampede of doubt. She couldn't bring herself to go into the saloon just yet, so she stalled in front of a plaque mounted at eye level on the Hill Country sandstone the old building had been constructed of. The historical plaque had been hung right next to the saloon door and near an odd smattering of fingertip-sized holes in the wall.

Taking deep, steadying breaths, she pretended to read the plaque, only gleaning that there had been a battle of some sort in 1836 and a *last stand*—thus, the town and saloon's name—was made here in the saloon. Explained the holes pockmarking the sandstone. They were bullet holes. This town was indeed her kind of place. A peaceful space born of chaos.

Hopefully, her last stand wouldn't occur here as well. But if it did, at least she could score a drink.

No. Sammie squared her shoulders. Not only would she have to pass on the liquor, but she also couldn't chicken out or fail. Her friends were counting on her. They believed in her. She'd tell herself that as many times as needed.

It was time for her to cowgirl up and get in there.

Pulling the long curls she'd styled her hair into over one shoulder, she took a second to check that she'd correctly buttoned her crisp, white cotton shirt embroidered with the Grit and Grace logo right over her heart before pushing her way through the saloon's heavy front door.

Sammie paused just inside, giving her eyes time to adjust to the difference between the comparatively bright light outside and the dim interior of the saloon. The stone the building had been constructed of had been left exposed on the interior, with booths lining the walls. A large booth in the corner, currently occupied by a handful of older men, caught Sammie's attention. But she wanted to be sure and not just make a wild guess. Several tables filled the middle space, some occupied by only men and some by men and women. Sammie wove her way past them to reach the bar.

As she waited for the bartender, a big, handsome man, to notice her, she checked out the rest of the place as subtly as she could. A framed line drawing of the saloon depicted its early days, either before or after the violence that had left the building riddled with bullet holes. Sammie couldn't tell. An alcove off to the side boasted a pool table and a jukebox, both currently unused.

The bartender replaced the glass he'd been drying and came her way. "What can I get you?"

Sammie didn't really want anything, afraid she'd spill it down her front, thanks to her nerves. Or worse, barf. Which she might do regardless, so she asked for a ginger ale to hopefully stave off the nausea.

With a quick nod he moved to snag a can of the soda from an undercounter refrigerator and popped the top, filled a tall glass with ice, then poured in the ginger ale.

When he returned and placed it in front of her, adding a straw, he gestured at the small logo sewn on her shirt. "You part of the group leasing the A Bar H?"

"I am."

He extended his hand. "Slater Highwater."

She shook his hand. "Sammie Abel."

"Nice to meet you, Sammie. Welcome to Last Stand."

The genuine warmth in his pleasantries bolstered Sammie's courage. She asked, "Could you do me a favor?"

"I'll try," he said with no small amount of charm.

"I'm looking for the Last Stand Rodeo officials. Regina Rhinehart told me they would be here?" While she felt the need to name-drop the only name she had, she stopped short of saying she had an appointment with them because... well, she didn't. She hoped to live here in Last Stand for the foreseeable future and didn't want to come out of the chute a liar.

He tipped his head toward the men in the corner booth who had initially caught her eye. "That's them."

"Thank you." Sammie smiled and pulled cash from her pocket and paid for her drink.

Gripping the glass of ginger ale with both hands, just in

case her jitters transferred to the liquid, Sammie made her way to the corner booth.

She could do this. *Fake it until you make it, darlin'.* The mantra had brought her this far and hopefully wouldn't let her down now.

Her shiny, smiley presence was enough to gain the men's attention, and their conversation evaporated as their gazes went to her.

She opened with, "I'm so sorry for interrupting, but Ms. Rhinehart said I could find y'all here tonight." Sort of. Not really. So much for not being a liar. But the fib couldn't be helped. She needed them to listen to her.

The man closest to her, probably in his late fifties, balding, and with a friendly smile said, "Then it's our lucky day. What can we do for you?"

"Grant me a few minutes of your time?"

The men exchanged quick, bemused glances that set Sammie's teeth on edge. By now she should be used to being patronized by men involved in both small, local rodeos, and rodeos not so small, but she still found the attitude irritating. Which was admittedly hypocritical. She was counting on her looks to get their attention, but she also needed them to see beyond her appearance and judge her by her brains and experience.

Luckily, she had good balance, or else she'd never be able to walk the tightrope women often had to traverse to get ahead in this world.

The same man said, "I suppose we can spare a few minutes."

On the chance he literally meant only a few minutes, Sammie swiftly seated herself at the end of the large corner booth table in a chair that had obviously been pulled over earlier from a nearby unoccupied table. She moved aside a half-empty glass of beer and replaced it with her own glass of ginger ale so she could fold her hands in faux tranquility atop the table. "Thank you so much, gentlemen."

There was a moment of elbow jabs and guffaws at being referred to so courteously.

Sammie waited for them to remember they were actually grown men before she launched into her sales pitch. "My name is Sammie Abel, co-owner of Grit and Grace Rodeo Roughstock Company. A local company operating out of the—"

The equally balding man seated across the booth from the first man who'd spoken said, "The A Bar H. Acquired a few years ago and totally renovated by the Halliday Oil Company heir, Asher Halliday. Yes, we know. Small town, and all."

Another man joined in. "The Buckin' Babes are famous in these parts. You've done a lot for women in rodeo, proving that cowgirls are just as tough as cowboys."

"Tougher," the man on her left who'd spoken first interjected.

"Tougher, yes." He chuckled. "Truly impressive that you

gals are stepping up to the rodeo roughstock game."

The other men nodded their agreement.

Sammie shifted forward in her seat. Interesting that they thought owning and contracting out bulls, broncs, and steers to rodeos was a step up from competing in ranch bronc riding. She let the comment slide without remark and went back to the pitch she'd rehearsed on the drive into town. "Thank you. We believe we are uniquely qualified to provide quality rough stock to well-run rodeos such as the one here in Last Stand. Not only do we have the practical experience riding broncs, but we have on board a bona fide geneticist—"

"But you were looking for investors, correct? Does that mean you don't have the funds to provide the rough stock that would be required now?"

"No, we do. Or at least we will, when the rest of the bulls and broncs we've acquired arrive in the next day or two. We are simply seeking funding for the future expansions we have planned." As well as to pay the current bills, but Sammie kept that part to herself.

The balding man on her left twirled his glass and mused, "Seed money from the Hallidays, rough stock from Thomas Wright . . . you ladies have connections, don't you?"

Surprise derailed Sammie for a second, then she forced herself to shrug, aiming for *what's a girl to do*? But she was momentarily taken aback by what they already knew. As the other balding man had said, *small town*. Plus, the rodeo-inclined investors the ladies had invited out to the A Bar H the other day had to know the local rodeo officials. The rodeo world was ultimately a small one. Everything made sense.

The question at hand, though, was did she lean into their assumptions about her and her friends' connections, which weren't entirely wrong, thanks to Peyton's generous family and fiancé, or did she try to steer them in the *we're making it on our own* direction?

As she engaged in a bout of mental tug-of-war, the oldest of the men, seated directly opposite her in the deepest bend of the U-shaped booth, spoke. "Connected or not, you and your fellow female bronc riders have brought the inclusive spirit of rodeo back. We applaud you."

To Sammie's horror, the men around the table did just that. Her face flamed hot while they clapped.

Despite the embarrassing display in front of her, Sammie sensed a presence directly behind her a second before a heavy hand settled on her shoulder.

A deep, familiar voice said, "Wherever Sammie Abel goes, applause follows."

The gentleman on her left said, "Sorry, Alec, but we found a prettier occupant for your seat."

The extra chair pulled up to the booth, the half-empty beer . . .

Realization hit Sammie like a dunk in an icy water trough and she bolted out of the chair, out from under his warm touch. "I am so sorry. Clearly, I interrupted *your* meeting with the Last Stand Rodeo officials."

Mortified that she'd thought for even a second that she could compete with the likes of Thomas Wright's spawn, no matter how far removed, Sammie started to back away from the table. From Alec. From the very real threat he represented to her future. To her heart.

Alec reached out and snagged hold of her biceps, halting her escape. Embarrassment kept her from meeting his blue gaze. Instead, she took in his hat-creased and finger-mussed blond hair, his black cotton button-down shirt with the Wright Ranch logo over his heart, his dark-washed pressed jeans, and his polished town boots. He'd dressed to impress, as well.

She tried to tug away from his grip as subtly as she could. When he didn't release his hold on her, mortification gave way to the hot simmer of anger.

How stupid would she be to run from this chance to make her pitch just because he'd been able to secure an actual meeting with them? How stupid would she be to simply hand him the contract by tucking tail and running? Worst of all, how stupid had she been to believe that maybe, just maybe, Alec had traveled all the way to Texas for her?

THE BITTER TASTE of guilt with a chaser of regret filled Alec's mouth as he watched the play of emotions pass across

Sammie's beautiful face. Especially when it became obvious the emotion that won out was anger.

Though, had he really thought he could win this roughstock contract for the Wright Ranch, for his grandfather, without torching any chance he might have had with Sammie? The women of Grit and Grace needed to start scoring contracts if they hoped to succeed. And while there was plenty of competition for rodeo roughstock contracts, some based right here in Last Stand and the surrounding area, few brought with them the tradition and clout of his grandfather.

Alec couldn't blame Sammie for being angry.

And she shouldn't be surprised that despite the guilt shredding his guts, he was as equally determined. He would prove himself to be more than just the baby of the family, always out for a wild ride and a good time, sometimes all at once. He would win this contract on his own, but he would give Grit and Grace an honest chance, as he would anyone. Mother of his child or not, he thought wryly.

Gene Bauer, the Last Stand Rodeo's arena director, cleared his throat. "Er, do you two need a moment?"

"No," Sammie almost snarled.

"Yes," Alec said at the same time.

The older man's eyebrows shot up. "I'd assumed you two were cooperators, with the girls being given Wright Ranch stock and all, but maybe I should be thinking of you as adversaries?"

Alec felt Sammie go stiff when Gene called her and her partners "girls," and by the time he'd finished speaking, she was positively vibrating and straining toward the door. Alec stepped a little closer to Sammie to keep her from either bolting or launching herself at the table of crusty old farts. "If you could give Miss Abel and I a moment, I'd appreciate it."

Sammie protested, "Alec, no. I—"

"Shh," he said in her ear and used his body to move her away from the table of now very curious men toward the door.

Gene called after them, "Alec, we would like an answer to our questions."

"I'll get back to you. Promise," Alec called over his shoulder but didn't stop herding Sammie out the door like the best cattle dog.

"Alec," Sammie protested, but he didn't stop until they were on the sidewalk in front of the saloon.

The moment he released her, Sammie whirled to face him. "Dammit, Alec, that was my one chance to get them to agree to accept a bid from Grit and Grace."

"I'll make sure you get another. I promise."

"You? Why? Why would you help me submit a bid when you are clearly only here to snag the contract yourself?"

"Because I think everyone should have a fair chance."

Blonde brows shot up. "A fair chance?"

"Yeah. You know, a level playing field."

"A level playing field?" Sammie barked out an incredulous laugh and stepped away from him. "Says the guy standing on the mountain his grandpa built."

The stark truth of her words hit him like a blunted horn between the eyes, knocking him back a step. He'd heard virtually the same accusation his entire life. His own anger flared, and he regained the step. "No. I'm going to do this on my own. On my own merits. I do know a thing or two about rough stock, and what a rodeo needs from their roughstock contractors."

She crossed her arms tightly over her chest. "Of course you do. Having grown up on a multi-million-dollar rodeo roughstock ranch."

"Yes. Where I worked my tail off. Mucking stalls, bucking hay, wrangling steers, and training bulls and broncs by letting them dump me on my head in the mud. I had to prove myself at every step. I'm still having to prove myself."

Sammie dropped her arms to her side and her expression softened.

Dammit. He didn't want her to pity him. He had been very fortunate. Aside from having to watch his mother take a decade to die after being trampled by his grandfather's prized bull, that is. But because of that horrible experience, his remaining family had grown very close, very supportive. To the point his lone sister had, for a hot minute, been determined to become a rodeo bullfighter to keep him safe when he'd decided to become a bull rider.

Sammie said, "So how, exactly, do you intend to level the playing field?"

"When you came into the saloon, I'd stepped away to call Ian."

"Your oldest brother, who runs the ranch."

"Yeah. I called him to confirm the stock we have available for the dates of the rodeo here."

She planted her hands on her hips. "Which levels the playing field how?"

"I also confirmed which stock was headed to the A Bar H." He eased closer to her. "Grandpa gave Drew quality animals to send to Grit and Grace."

"And that's how you're leveling the playing field," she stated, rather than asked.

He tucked a silky blonde curl behind her ear. "As much as I can, against a group of smart, capable women with more courage in their little fingers than most men could pretend to have in their whole bodies."

Sammie rolled her eyes. "Get back in there and finish your pitch."

She turned away and walked to her truck, but Alec didn't miss the tiny smile tugging at her lush mouth.

He couldn't suppress his huge grin as he went back into the Last Stand Saloon. While he couldn't do much about the fact that he and Sammie were competitors, he'd make damn sure they weren't adversaries.

Chapter Six

SAMMIE SQUINTED AGAINST the glare of the low evening sun flashing intermittently through the leafy canopy of live oaks and hickory, with mesquite and pecan trees filling the space below. She gripped the truck's steering wheel so tightly her hands ached. Not because the road between Last Stand and the A Bar H was busy or difficult to drive. Just the opposite. The road easily wound through the pastoral, gently rolling hills still splashed with the vibrant colors of lavender. Flowers Sammie barely noticed at all.

She was strangling the wheel because she was mad. Mad at the good ol' boys who were born and bred to only see her as hair and lip gloss. Mad at the culture that rewarded them. Mad at the world for merrily spinning around while she'd been so soundly knocked off kilter.

Mad at Alec, of course, for being the one to send her off axis, even before she'd discovered she carried his child. But most of all, she was mad at herself. Because the decisions made were hers, either consciously made or not. Ultimately, the buck stopped with her.

Her gaze was drawn to the grocery bag on the seat next to her. Within were all sorts of bad decisions. But turns out, pregnancy cravings were real. So real.

Sammie peeled one hand off the steering wheel and reached into the bag, rooting around until her hand closed around the package of soft, squishy goodness. She pulled out the hand-sized half-orb of cream-filled chocolate cake covered with marshmallow frosting and pink coconut flakes. God bless small-town markets, where childhood favorites abounded.

Using her teeth, she ripped the plastic wrapper off, sending coconut down her front. She didn't care. All that mattered to Sammie was getting rid of the awful ache behind her breastbone she was choosing to call hunger.

If the sweet treat didn't do the trick, there were dill pickle-flavored potato chips in the bag too. They were a little too on the nose when it came to appeasing pregnancy cravings, but she didn't care. They simply sounded good to her.

Just like her plan for tonight had sounded good. It had been good. How was she to know a meeting with Alec was the reason for the local rodeo officials being at the saloon this evening? Despite Alec's presence she should have pushed to make her pitch anyhow. But she hadn't, so she'd simply have to try yet again to get an actual appointment with the officials. If she couldn't, she'd be forced to bump into them again. Somehow.

She took a bite of the cream-filled cake. She could always

mail in a formal bid, or hand deliver one, but guessing the right number without being able to feel out what the rodeo could afford to pay for the rough stock would be tough.

Of course, she could always ask Alec what he intended to bid, then simply bid lower. Arguably, any loss Grit and Grace sustained on their first contract would be worth it to get a foot in the rodeo roughstock game. But she'd have to clear offering up a low bid with her partners. Just as she'd have to get Alec to tell her his bid.

So much for avoiding him. She took an aggressive bite of cake.

Sammie had eaten halfway through the domed sweet when the truck sputtered. She looked down at the dashboard and for the first time noticed the little illuminated gas pump symbol meant to warn the driver of a low gas level in the tank. The indicator was red. Very red. And the needle on the gas gauge sat firmly on the equally red line next to the big letter, "*E*." *E* for empty.

"Oh no," Sammie sputtered around the massive bite of cake she'd just taken.

Laura had warned Sammie to fill the truck with gas from the pump used to fuel up the ranch's vehicles and equipment, but she'd completely forgotten. She'd been too consumed with what she'd say to the Last Stand Rodeo officials when she crashed their meeting. Nor had she noticed the gas gauge edging to empty once she arrived in town, let alone before she left Last Stand in a huff.

The truck's engine sputtered again, then again, before coughing to a stop. She swallowed down the suddenly dry bite of chocolate cake.

"Oh no," Sammie repeated as she steered the truck to the narrow shoulder on the side of the road. "Great. Just great." She'd have to call one of the girls to come rescue her with a can of gas.

First, though, she'd finish off the cake.

After popping the last delicious bite in her mouth, she searched her pockets for her cell phone, then remembered she'd placed it on the passenger seat beneath the bag of junk food she'd bought. She leaned to feel under the bag, inadvertently dumping the bag's contents out onto the seat, relaxing when her hand closed over the phone.

A knock sounded on the driver's side window.

Sammie jumped, her heart in her throat, and turned toward the noise.

Alec *Freakin'* Neisson, his knuckles still raised as if he'd have to knock on the window again. What had he thought she was doing on the side of the road? Taking a nap? She glanced in the rearview mirror. A big, shiny black truck was parked directly behind her and she hadn't even noticed.

His brows went up and he called through the shut window, "Sammie? You okay?"

Painfully aware of the bag of wildly unhealthy snacks partially dumped on the seat next to her, Sammie unfastened her seatbelt and opened the truck door. He took a step back so she could climb from the truck. While she didn't expect any traffic, she still looked both ways before getting out. The road was empty as far as the eye could see. Except for her and Alec. She left the truck door open and leaned against it in a bid for nonchalance.

"You okay?" he said again. "Why are you stopped?"

She heaved a sigh and took her medicine. "Ran out of gas."

He blinked. "Seriously?"

"Yes, I'm serious. Laura had mentioned I needed to fill the truck's tank before I left the ranch, but I forgot to do it."

She waited for the laughter, for jibes, to be made fun of for being a ditzy blonde. Maybe even to be hit on, since it was just the two of them on a deserted road surrounded by a sea of fading purple flowers.

Instead, Alec put his hands on his hips and glowered at her. "You need to be more careful."

"Excuse me?"

"You're pregnant, Sammie. You need to be more careful. If something were to happen—"

"I didn't go bungee jumping, Alec. I ran out of gas. And I certainly didn't do it on purpose."

"Is there something wrong with the gauge?" He moved past her to look at the dash.

Trapped between Alec's lean, muscular body and the open truck door, Sammie tried to press herself back away from him, but she was still enveloped by the heat and heavenly spicy smell that was Alec Neisson. The excess hormones in her body clamored for contact with him, especially when the very vivid memory of how those muscles had felt beneath her fingers and what that spicy heat tasted like flashed through her.

"No," she practically squeaked. "There's nothing wrong with the gas gauge. At least I don't think so. Like I said, I just forgot to refill the tank with gas."

Alec grunted in response and started to lean back out of the truck. Sammie could tell when he noticed the spilled bag of junk food on the passenger seat because he stilled for a moment before straightening. But he remained in her space. Unintentionally crowding her. Or maybe not so unintentionally. His bright-blue gaze drifted downward, and a smile tugged at his mouth.

Before she could guess what he found amusing, he reached up and picked something off the front of her shirt, right above her right breast. He held up a small, pink-tinted chunk of coconut between his fingers and raised a blond brow.

Heat flooded her cheeks, and she quickly brushed at her shirt and wiped at her mouth, imagining chunks of creamy chocolate cake stuck to her face.

His smile widened. "Let me guess . . . cravings?"

"What do you know of cravings?" she groused, annoyed by her embarrassment. Annoyed by the man's beauty. Annoyed by how his smile tugged at that thing behind her breastbone.

"My sister Caitlin. She ate the weirdest things when she was pregnant. Like barbeque potato chips mixed in with ice cream. Didn't matter what flavor of ice cream, either. I once watched her dump almost an entire bag of barbeque chips on a bowl of strawberry ice cream and just stir it all together." He shuddered.

While Sammie seriously considered the possible merits of the combination, Alec considered the pink flake he'd picked off her for a brief moment before popping it into his mouth.

"Ah, coconut. Wait. Did you find one of those snowball cake thingies? Man, I loved those as a kid. My oldest brother, Ian, used to take Drew and me to the little market in Pineville to buy them. Don't they come in a two-pack?" His attention shifted back into the truck, clearly planning to mooch her goodies.

Sammie wasn't having it. She stretched an arm across the opening to grip the opposite edge of the truck's door frame and block his access to the cab. "Do you have extra gas or not? Because if you don't, I need to call home—" She realized with a jolt that she did think of the A Bar H Ranch as home already. She liked having a place that felt like home. She didn't want to lose it.

He stepped away from her with a sigh. "Let me just drive you to the ranch. Justin and I will come back later with gas."

Sammie's first inclination was to argue. She and her friends had set out on this journey with the intention of doing it all on their own. Without needing, or wanting, to be rescued by hunky cowboys. But a wave of exhaustion broke over her. Maybe just this time, she'd let a particularly hunky cowboy do her a favor. And maybe she could use the time to extract some information from him. Yeah, that'd work.

"Fine. Do you think the truck will be okay here?"

"I won't let it sit here long. And there's not much traffic other than those coming and going from the A Bar H."

Sammie nodded and started gathering her things from the truck's cab, shoving everything into the plastic bag from the store. She locked and shut the truck's door.

Alec hovered, extending a hand for the bag.

She waved him off. "I got it." She wanted to tell him she was pregnant, not infirm. But considering his adherence to the cowboy way, he'd offer to carry anything and everything for her simply because it was the gentlemanly thing to do, regardless of her physical state.

Case in point, he hustled to the passenger door of his truck and held it open for her.

Because she didn't completely hate the courtesy, she muttered her thanks and started to climb into the truck. She paused. "Wait. This isn't the same truck you had before. Did you have to get a new rental?"

"This one's mine."

"What do you mean?"

"I returned the rental and bought this one. With you and

I having a—" His gaze flicked to her stomach. "Baby on board, I'll need a vehicle here in Texas. Made sense to buy one instead of renting. Do you like it?"

No, she didn't like it. Not only did the high-end, clearly loaded truck represent their economic differences—she'd had to save for years to buy a total beater—it represented Alec Neisson's permanent presence in her life. But there was nothing more permanent than his baby, so there was that.

All she could do was shrug. "Does it have gas?"

"Yes."

"Then I like it."

Alec eyed her as if he'd just let a badger into his new truck as he swung the door shut.

Sammie pretended she hadn't noticed, busying herself with settling the bag of snacks on the floorboard between her feet, buckling her seatbelt, and trying her best to ignore the fact that despite it being brand-new, the cab already smelled like Alec—spicy aftershave, saddle leather, and the open range. Or maybe Alec just had a new truck smell. She'd believe anything at this point.

Alec rounded the truck and climbed into the driver's seat. After a not-so-subtle check to see that she'd buckled her seatbelt, he reached for his own seatbelt and winced.

Sammie grimaced in empathy. "What did Drew say about your shoulder?"

"Same thing as the sports medicine docs in Fort Worth said right after it happened. The only way it will heal is to rest it. So here I am, resting."

"Only a cowboy would consider bucking hay, digging postholes, and hoisting saddles resting."

He glanced at her. "You been keeping track of me?"

A little. "No." *Okay, a lot.* "I just know what Justin had scheduled to work on this week, and since you're helping him . . ." She shrugged to imply her assumptions were obvious ones.

Alec smirked as he started the truck, turned down the country music radio station he'd been listening to, and put the gear shift into drive. "You've totally been watching me."

Sammie opened her mouth to protest, then stopped herself. What was the point? As long as they were both living on the same ranch, no matter how sprawling, she would be aware of him. As long as they lived on the same planet, she would be aware of him.

Alec eased the truck onto the road and started them toward the ranch. "But I am not riding bulls. Which equals resting for me."

"For how long?"

He turned to look pointedly at her. "Depends."

"On?"

"You, of course."

Her heart stuttered, then raced. What in the heck did he mean? And what had she expected him to say? That his going back to the bull riding circuit depended on how well he healed? On whether he reinjured himself simply living the ranch life, like while mucking stalls? Or on his securing the Last Stand Rodeo roughstock contract and his grandfather rewarding him by making him her full-time competitor?

Sammie pressed her lips together and shifted her focus out the window. She could feel his gaze on her.

"Have you seen a doctor yet?"

Everything in her wanted to throw up a wall between them, to shut him out. Keeping him at arm's length would be the only way to avoid being hurt.

But it was too late for that. He was the father of her unborn child.

And she had a rodeo roughstock contract bid number to sleuth out.

ALEC HELD HIS breath, waiting for Sammie to respond. Maybe he shouldn't have brought up the subject. She'd brought up doctors, though, when asking about his shoulder and her and their baby's well-being had been on his mind. Would continue to be until . . . well, forever.

The thought knocked the breath from his lungs more effectively than a hoof to the diaphragm.

He forced his lungs to expand again. With Sammie and a child in his life, he'd have to get used to the worry, annoyance, and frustration. Just as he'd grown used to something on his body being stiff, hurt, or downright broken after deciding he wanted to compete as a pro bull rider.

She heaved a sigh and shifted in his new truck's passenger seat. "I have not seen a doctor. I wanted to help get everything settled on the ranch first."

"Isn't it important to be checked out pretty early in the pregnancy?"

He shifted his gaze to her in time to see her shrug in response. "I don't know."

He looked back at the road. Here came the frustration, tightening his chest and his grip on the steering wheel. He pulled in a couple more calming breaths. "Have you at least looked for someone to see here in Last Stand? I know they have a hospital and everything. So that's good."

"Yeah. It'll be fine. I'll find someone, and it'll be fine."

He quickly glanced at her as he drove through the elaborately scrolled wrought iron entrance to the A Bar H, his tires vibrating over the cattle guard. She was staring straight ahead, her jaw set.

He was swamped with the need to help her as he returned his gaze to the drive. "I can call around and find someone for you—"

"No," she cut him off sharply, then softened. "Really, I got this. But thanks."

"Sure." He slowed his speed, not wanting her to be able to escape him just yet. "Can I come?"

"What?"

"Can I come with you when you go to see the doctor?"

"Alec—" There was a ton of warning in her tone.

He didn't care. "Seriously, Sammie. I want to be a part of this process."

"Process? I've never heard a pregnancy called a process."

"You're building a human being. What else would it be besides a process?"

Sammie groaned and pressed a hand to her stomach. "Please, Alec. I'm not ready yet."

"To see a doctor? I don't think—"

"No. For people to know."

"That you're pregnant?"

"That you're the father."

The admission brought him up short. "Why?"

"Just for now, Alec. Okay?"

He wanted to argue with her, to push for her to tell the world they were going to have a baby together, but with everything else happening, namely the rodeo contract they were both pursuing, he'd give her this. "Okay. But the doctor will need to know, so it'll make sense for me to be—"

"Why will the doctor need to know?"

"My medical history, insurance—"

She raised her hands in surrender. "All right. Just don't tell anyone else."

"I won't." *For now.*

She let out a noisy breath as he steered his truck into the main house's circular drive. "Are you going to the bunkhouse to write up the Wright Ranch bid now?"

"I have to crunch some numbers first, but yes."

Sammie twisted in the captain's seat to face him fully, her blue eyes intense. "Can I come and watch?"

Alarm bells went off in Alec's head.

Chapter Seven

SAMMIE STUDIED ALEC'S face beneath the brim of his pristine white cowboy hat, his blue eyes crystalline in the glaringly bright light of the low Texas sun shining through the truck's front windshield. His handsome features revealed nothing of his thoughts about her request to watch him put together the Wright Ranch's bid for the Last Stand's rodeo roughstock contract.

He appeared to be studying her as intensely. She willed herself to remain still, praying she was hiding her thoughts as well as he was, but she feared her anxiety and desperation might be leaking into her gaze or was evident in the unintended tightness of her mouth. She started racking her brain for another excuse that would allow her a peek at his numbers when he finally spoke.

"Yeah, all right." He gestured at the arched double front doors of the main house. "Do you want to let the others know where you are?"

"I'll text them." She shifted in the passenger's captain seat and leaned forward to fish her phone out of the plastic shopping bag where she'd tossed it. "I'll let them know about the truck running out of gas too. So they won't wonder."

"Good call." Alec eased his truck out of the main house's circular drive and turned toward the bunkhouse, located near the horse barn and corral.

Her phone in her hand, Sammie debated what to text Laura, who'd known what Sammie had traveled to town to do. She settled on the truth. Mostly.

Was able to speak with the rodeo officials. Went well. But truck ran out of gas on way back—guess who forgot to fill the tank—Alec gave me a ride back and agreed to show me how to write up bid. At bunkhouse if needed.

Sammie hesitated a moment, debating the message, but when, out of the corner of her eye, she caught Alec glancing at her, she hit SEND.

Laura responded almost immediately.

Woot! You rock! I knew you'd get the contract. Do we need to go after the truck?

Sammie's mouth filled with the bitter taste of shame, and the temptation to correct Laura's assumption about the contract almost overwhelmed her. But she would get the contract, so she wouldn't be misleading her friends. At least, not for long.

She looked at Alec as he parked his truck next to the vehicles belonging to Justin and the other ranch hand employed full time by Asher Halliday. "Are you sure Justin won't mind going after the ranch truck with you?"

"If he can't, Carlos will. It's no biggie." He put the truck in PARK and turned the engine off.

"Thank you," Sammie said before responding to Laura's text.

Alec and Justin will get the truck.

As Alec was climbing from the truck, Sammie's phone buzzed with another text from Laura.

K. If you aren't back to the main house in time for dinner, I'll make up a plate and put it in the fridge.

While she wasn't sure how hungry she'd be after her snack attack, Sammie sent back a quick *thank you* text just as the truck's passenger door opened and Alec reached in to take the grocery bag from the floorboard between her feet. She might as well let him.

Then he offered her his free hand to help her out of the truck. Sammie balked, more than capable of getting out of a truck on her own, but she reminded herself she needed him complacent, so she played along.

She placed her hand in his and instantly regretted the tactic as electricity raced up her arm. His palm was rough and hot against hers. His grip strong, but infinitely gentle.

Memories of their night together assaulted her both visually and physically. Sweat erupted between her breasts as he supported her while she climbed from the tall truck. And when he didn't step back, instead remaining in her space as he looked down into her eyes, she went up in flames.

Being so near to Alec for any amount of time was dangerous business. She was still so incredibly attracted to him. Combined with his chivalrous nature and seemingly genuine concern for her well-being, she was reminded all over again of why she'd ghosted him. He would be so easy to fall for. And then she would end up just like her mother and grandmother, who'd had no lives of their own. Not that Sammie knew what her mom's life was really like, but based on what her grandmother said, Sammie wasn't wrong.

She needed to discover the bid number he intended to give the local rodeo officials, though, so she'd have to risk the assault on her hormones. She couldn't allow herself to get sucked in by his charisma or the chemistry that clearly continued to spark between them.

Most importantly, she had to stay out of his bedroom.

Her mouth dry as a Texas summer, she broke away from Alec's gaze, slipped her hand from his, and stepped around him. She busied herself with tucking her phone into her back pocket as he shut the truck door and led the way to the bunkhouse entrance.

Constructed of the same multi-colored sandstone and dark-stained rough-hewn timber as the main house, the bunkhouse was equally welcoming. In a high-end sort of way. Sammie had yet to see inside the T-shaped building. Laura had been the one entrusted to tour the property with Peyton and her oldest brother, Asher, the owner, before they signed the lease. Because the bunkhouse was already occupied by Justin and the other hands, Sammie, and as far as she knew, the other girls, hadn't checked it out when they'd arrived at the ranch.

Alec opened the door and stepped aside to allow Sammie to enter first. She walked into what turned out to be a lovely great room with a modern kitchen to the left and a seating area to the right with pale hardwood floors throughout. She was hit with a wall of cool, air-conditioned air, saturated with the smell of cooking peppers that brought her up short.

Her stomach rebelled and the sweet snack cake she'd scarfed down earlier threatened to make a reappearance. Alec's light touch on her back eased her forward, making room for him to enter also and close the door behind them. Sammie breathed slowly and deeply through her mouth to keep from being sick.

"Hey," Justin called without turning from where he stood in front of the stove, obviously cooking the source of the stomach-turning—at least for her—smell.

"Hey," Alec said back.

"How'd it go?" Justin asked, then turned toward them and his thickly lashed hazel eyes went wide. "Oh. Ms. Abel." He moved the pan off the heat and grabbed a dish towel to wipe his hands. "What do you need? Is there something I can do for you?"

Carlos, the ranch hand who mostly looked after the longhorns, popped up from the dark-brown leather sectional, where he'd been watching a baseball game on the huge flat-screen TV mounted on the wall. He hurriedly tucked his light-blue cambric shirt back into his jeans.

A blast of guilt and embarrassment took Sammie's mind off her nausea. She should have thought this plan through. Interrupting these hardworking men in their private space wasn't cool.

"Please, call me Sammie. And no, there's nothing," she rushed to reassure him.

"Aside from the ranch truck," Alec interjected. "Are you going to be around after dinner, Justin?"

"Sure am," Justin nodded, clearly curious.

"The ranch truck ran out of gas a couple of miles down the road. Can you run me down to get it in a bit?" Alec asked.

He didn't say she'd been driving the truck and had been the one to fail to fill the tank before she left. Ever the gentleman. She used to revel in such courtesies, so foreign to how she'd been treated in her grandmother's house, but now she found herself always looking for the motivation.

Justin frowned. "That's weird. I didn't think it was that low. And don't worry about it. Carlos and I can take care of it after we eat."

Sammie glanced at Carlos, and he was nodding emphatically. Her embarrassment grew. "I'm so sorry to disturb you guys."

"It's no problem," Justin said.

At the same time, Carlos said, "It's fine. No worries."

Moving farther into the room, Alec said, "Thanks, guys.

I'm going to show Ms. Abel how the Wright Ranch puts together a rodeo roughstock bid."

Sammie didn't miss the fact that Alec referred to her formally. Was it his not-so-subtle way of countering her insistence the men who worked the ranch call her by her preferred name?

Justin's sable brows shot up, and he exchanged a quick glance with Carlos. Then he shrugged. "Sounds good. No reason not to learn how the big dogs do it." Justin gestured at the pan he'd just taken off the heat. "I've made more than enough poblanos. How about some grub before you get to work?"

Sammie must have made a distressed sound because Alec planted his hand on the small of her back and urged her toward the long hall that started directly opposite the front door.

"Thanks for the offer, Justin," Alec said as he gently guided her to the hall. "But you guys go ahead. We have food." He lifted the plastic bag from the market and Sammie prayed it wasn't transparent enough to expose the junk food she'd bought. "And I have my laptop with the bid templates on it already set up in my room. Holler if you need anything."

Justin made a shooing motion. "No. Don't worry about us. You go."

The knowing grin on Justin's handsome face sent heat sluicing into Sammie's face. Great. Now Justin and Carlos would think she was having an affair with Alec Neisson. They'd already had their one-night affair. And Sammie was living with the consequence.

There were three doors on each side of the long hall, with what looked to be an exterior door at the very end. Alec opened the second door on the right, revealing a surprisingly spacious room dominated by a bed with a heavy timber headboard and footboard. A matching dresser occupied one wall with a saddle rack and plush reading chair, ottoman, and a side table on the opposite side of the bed. A decent-sized flat-screen TV was mounted on the wall facing the foot of the bed.

Nowhere was a set-up laptop to be seen.

"This is nice," she said.

Alec closed the door and placed the bag of snacks on the dresser. "It is. Asher has good taste."

"Or his interior designer does. Where's your computer?"

He removed his cowboy hat and hung it on a peg next to his work cowboy hat, then picked up a brown leather backpack from the floor next to the dresser. "Here." He unzipped the backpack and pulled out a thin laptop.

"Not set up," she stated rather than asked.

"No. But I had the feeling that if you stayed out there, smelling cooking poblanos, you'd be puking snowballs within five minutes."

Sammie put a hand beneath her nose, still picking up a faint whiff of peppers. "You are not wrong. But you know they'll think we're up to something in here."

Alec shrugged as if he couldn't care less and sat on the bed. He opened the laptop and powered it up. Patting the spot next to him, he said, "Have a seat."

She hesitated. Not only was she in Alec's current bedroom—nicer than the one in his fifth wheel—but he was inviting her to sit next to him on his bed. Which he'd impeccably made. What was she thinking, being here?

He looked up at her. "Are you still feeling sick? There's a garbage can behind you, right next to the door."

"No. I'm okay now."

When she remained rooted to her spot, he raised a blond brow at her. "Do you want to see how we put together a bid or not?"

"I do." She *needed* to, so she forced herself to move, pulling her phone from her back pocket and put it in her snack bag, then sat next to him on the bed.

The heat, the strength, the sex appeal rolling off Alec made it hard for Sammie to breathe and she found herself fisting her hands together in her lap.

Seemingly oblivious to her struggle, Alec shifted the computer on his lap so she could easily see the screen. Reminding herself, again, why she was here, Sammie did her damnedest to focus on what she was looking at.

As Alec had told Justin, he was showing her a template of a rodeo roughstock contract bid.

Minus any numbers.

Sammie could feel herself deflate, losing both energy and enthusiasm.

Alec pointed at the screen and started talking about the different aspects of the contract like the number of bulls, broncs, steers, and calves that would be provided to the rodeo, as well as the number of flankmen—or flankwomen, in her case—who would be made available to pull the flank straps on the bucking animals in the chutes, and so on.

He scrolled the document upward and pointed at the screen. "And here's where you put your bid number, which you arrive at by calculating how much your transportation costs, the manpower needed, feed for the duration of the rodeo, that kind of thing." He went through the entire document, explaining every element and the reasons behind its inclusion. He trailed off and looked at her expectantly.

When she continued to stare at the blank space where the final number would be, desperately trying to figure out how she would ever underbid him without any clue what number he would be quoting, he added, "I can email this template to you, if you'd like."

He was so sweet. And so infuriating.

"Thanks. That would be great." She gave him her email address and watched as he forwarded the form to her.

"Hey, you okay?" he asked softly. She could tell by his tone he wasn't referring to her upset stomach.

"Just tired. The fact I'm sitting on a bed—" *Your bed.* "Doesn't help."

He set his laptop on the nightstand. "You could..." He gestured behind them, at the plump pillows and suede-soft comforter.

"No. No, no, no... She started to get up.

Alec's warm hand closing over hers on the bed between them stopped her.

"Sammie, wait," he said softly, as if calming a frightened foal.

She settled back into her spot on the bed and stilled. The part of her that she was forever running from, the part of her constantly worrying she would never be enough, wanted desperately to hear what he had to say. She met his bright-blue gaze and was pulled in the same way she had been the night they'd slow-danced after the rodeo in Pineville, Oregon, five weeks ago.

His tone still gentle, he said, "I don't regret what happened between us. At all. For any reason. Please don't shut me out."

Sammie's heart begged for the chance to open to him, to let him in. Her brain knew better. He could literally take everything from her. She had to stay strong to stay independent, to stay in control of her and her baby's lives.

But as her brain cataloged the reasons why Alec was a bad idea, her gaze had dropped to the temptation that was his mouth. Firm yet soft, masculine yet so giving. By the time she realized she was leaning toward him, his free hand was slipping into her hair and anchoring her for his kiss.

The touch of his lips on hers, light at first, melted her resolve. Seeming to sense her surrender, no matter how momentary, Alec deepened the kiss and Sammie's entire being lightened, rising to meet him.

Her response to him had nothing to do with logic or rationality and everything to do with his pull on her. He was everything she'd ever wanted, but knew, in her soul, she could never have.

Much like at the beginning of their only night together, she didn't care.

A low moan erupted from somewhere deep within Sammie and she mirrored Alec by burying her hand in the short hair at the base of his head, holding him to her.

Holding him dear.

For now.

FIREWORKS EXPLODED IN Alec's head—and all points south—when Sammie met his tentative, hopeful kiss with her own hot passion. They were right together. So, so right.

He understood her need for autonomy, for independence, and he respected that need. The only problem was they were connected. By more than just her pregnancy. They fit together. Alec wanted nothing more than to find out in just how many ways.

She opened her mouth to him, and when his tongue

found hers, his brain shut down. He started to ease her back to lie on his bed when a loud knock sounded on his door.

Sammie jerked away from him like she'd grabbed hold of an electric fence on a dewy morning. She bolted to her feet right as the door, which he'd left unlocked like an idiot, opened.

Justin, with Carlos hovering at his back, stepped in without preamble. "Alec—" Justin stopped, taking in what had to be an obviously awkward moment, with Alec half lying on the bed and Sammie standing next to him, her beautiful face flaming.

Clearly shaking off any implications of what he was seeing, Justin continued, "Carlos and I went to get the truck."

Sammie took a not-too-subtle step away from the bed. "Already? What about your dinner?"

"We're fast eaters," Justin said, then refocused on Alec. "Like I said, we went to get the truck, but when we started to add gas to the tank from the can we'd brought, we heard gas pouring out of the tank onto the pavement under the truck. I got a flashlight and crawled under to have a look-see, and I found this." He held up a long, red-handled screwdriver.

Alec sat up straight, the fog of passion evaporating from his brain. "Where?"

"Buried hilt-deep in the gas tank. We had to tow the truck back here."

Sammie looked between them. "Could I have run over it and flicked it up in a way that it hit the gas tank? Or maybe the screwdriver dropped through from the truck bed to the gas tank when I hit a bump or something?"

Alec met Justin's hazel eyes and saw the same doubt that was clamoring through his brain. "Maybe. Check the other vehicles."

Justin tipped his head to Carlos, who nodded in agreement, then quickly headed back down the hall.

As Justin reached to close the bedroom door, Alec said, "I'll come help in a second."

Justin gave a quick lift of his chin in acknowledgement, then shut the door.

Sammie spread her arms wide. "What?"

While he wanted to be straight with her, there was no way he was going to worry the mother of his unborn child. "It's okay. We just need to be sure there are no other wayward tools that could have been run over."

Or anyone in town, where Sammie had left the truck unattended, who had a thing against women trying to make a go of it in the rodeo roughstock world.

Chapter Eight

As the sun dipped below the horizon and the cicadas, katydids, and crickets escalated their nightly serenade, Sammie made her way along the narrow flagstone path from the bunkhouse to the main house. Alec walked directly behind her, carrying the bag of snacks. He'd insisted on accompanying her, and she was a bundle of nerves, anticipating him bringing up what had happened between them in his room.

He'd kissed her.

Worse, she'd kissed him back. And the sensations, the connection, had been even more wonderful than when they had first kissed in Pineville. That first night had been all about giving in to passion, about discovery. Tonight, the fire fueling their kiss pulled from something deeper, more profound.

Then they'd almost been caught by the ranch manager and a ranch hand. She could still feel the sting of mortification in her cheeks from the near miss of her and Alec being found out as being . . . something. She didn't know what to call what she shared with Alec. Besides parenthood, that is. Thankfully, Justin and Carlos hadn't lingered in Alec's doorway after delivering the news of their discovery of the screwdriver-punctured gas tank.

The two men were currently peering under the rest of the vehicles, looking for any other *wayward* tools. Justin had been checking his own truck when she and Alec left the bunkhouse. Alec had paused long enough to tell Justin he would be right back, and Sammie told him the search could wait until morning, but Justin said he wouldn't be able to sleep until he made sure gas wasn't leaking from any other vehicle.

She knew she should be putting more thought into how the gas tank on the truck she'd been driving had ended up with a screwdriver jammed into it, but her brain was overwhelmed by Alec's kiss.

He'd rocked her world. Again. Right on the heels of asking her not to shut him out.

Only she had to protect herself. As soon as the couple of bulls and broncs from the Wright Ranch arrived, he'd certainly return home to Oregon, regardless of what he said he intended to do. His family, his home, was in Pineville. As was his future. Before their night together, when everything between them had been nothing but flirty fun, he'd told her he hoped to one day be able to take over the Wright Ranch's bucking bull program from his grandfather.

Probably sooner rather than later, considering how hard

competitive bull riding was on his body. Plus, his grandfather wasn't exactly a spring chicken. Alec had said he wanted him to be able to retire and enjoy the fruits of decades of hard work.

She didn't doubt for a second that Alec intended to be a part of their child's life. With three brothers and a sister, his father and grandfather, all incredibly close, from what she could tell, family was everything to him. What she did doubt was his intention to stay here in Last Stand with Sammie. The odds were with him wanting to take her baby back to Oregon with him. Where would that leave her?

Sammie couldn't allow him to break her heart and take her baby. She had to stand strong against his allure and keep him at arm's length. Falling for Alec would only lead to heartache. Weren't her mother's and grandmother's track records proof enough that nothing lasted?

On cue, his strong, warm hand settled low on her back, as if to steady her as she climbed the three stone steps leading to the main house's gated back patio and pool area. Alec stepped around her to open the chest-high, black, wrought iron gate, holding it open for her to walk through. She studiously ignored him as she went by. But it was an effort. The man had a strong magnetic pull. If she weren't careful, she'd find herself drawn into his orbit, where she'd lose all sense of herself.

On an automatic timer, the pool and attached hot tub, walkway, and yard lights clicked on, illuminating the densely planted, drought-resistant landscaping and the irregularly shaped free-form pool and hot tub. The nighttime bug chorus went silent for a beat, then began again in unison. Nature seemed to enjoy the oasis Asher Halliday had created as much as the women of Grit and Grace did after long days spent setting up their operation.

Sammie had almost reached the rear door to the main house that opened directly into a mudroom combined with a laundry room when Alec said softly, "Sammie?"

The temptation to keep going, to escape into the house where she could pretend nothing had changed, that she had control of her life, was strong. But she had kissed him back tonight. She should think of the moment with regret, but the warmth still buzzing low in her belly prevented her from doing so. Boundaries needed to be set, though, if he continued to hang around. There would be no more kissing. This was as good a time as any to tell him as much.

She turned to face him in the low light. His expression was shadowed by the brim of his cowboy hat, but his height, broad shoulders, and loose-limbed stance made her heart give a little bump.

She fisted her hands against his allure. "Look, Alec, what happened just now in your room was a mistake."

"Kissing you is never a mistake, Sammie."

Sammie's breath stalled in her chest. His statement was a loaded one, full of promise. But also one she couldn't trust. She could easily find herself yearning for something she knew wouldn't be good for her.

Alec subtly shifted toward her. "That's not what I wanted to talk about, though."

Still thrown off by his casually stated lack of regret, Sammie could only say, "Oh. What, then?"

"There might be men out there who are not okay with having to compete against women for rodeo roughstock contracts—"

To start the process of pushing him away, she blithely said, "Like you?"

"Me?" He rocked back on his boot heels. "Seriously? You really think that badly of me?"

Shame for her petulance flooded her. "No. I'm sorry." She blew out a breath and pushed her hair back from her face. "I'd love to blame . . ." She gestured at the unexpected occupant she was carrying and lowered her voice. "But despite the urge to barf all the time, I can't say that it even feels real yet, you know?"

He lifted a shoulder. "As much as any guy can, I guess."

Sammie tilted her head back to look at the endless, star-filled sky and found herself admitting, "I'm mostly just stressed."

"About . . .?" He mimicked her womb-encompassing gesture.

Appreciating his avoidance of the word pregnancy, she smiled. "Obviously. But also about not letting my friends down."

"Which leads us back to what I wanted to talk to you about."

"Right. You were saying?"

"That there might be some guy—not me—who doesn't think women should be doing what you all are doing. My point is, on the off chance the screwdriver to the gas tank wasn't a freak accident—"

Sammie drew her chin back in surprise. "You believe someone—some guy—crawled under the ranch truck, which technically belongs to Asher Halliday, and stuck a screwdriver in its gas tank as a form of protest against a group of women starting their own rodeo roughstock company?" Great. Something else to keep her up at night. But she and her friends were made of stronger stuff.

Alec spread his hands wide. "Trust me, men have been known to do stupider things."

"I won't argue with that. Seriously, though, even if what happened was basic misogyny, you don't have to worry. We can handle it. There were plenty of men who didn't think women were even capable of successfully riding broncs, ranch saddle or not, let alone that we should be allowed to compete at rodeos. We know exactly how to put them in their place."

"How?"

The burn of determination heated her blood. "By succeeding. By doing the very thing they say we can't and doing it well."

He started shaking his head before she'd finished. "Admirable strategy, but it doesn't address the whack jobs who might take things too far."

A thread of icy trepidation cooled her blood at the thought of her friends, her *baby*, being hurt. "What do you suggest?"

"Not to get caught out by yourselves. Make sure you always have one of us guys around."

She groaned. Of course, his solution would be to rely on him and the other men on the ranch. "You're joking, right? You think us delicate little flowers need big strong men to keep us safe? Clearly, you've never seen Meira practicing her Krav Maga."

"No, I haven't. But what about Laura, Beth, and Emma? What about you, Sammie?"

"I happen to wield a mean stall-mucking pitchfork."

"Humor me, Sammie. Please?"

The earnestness of his tone gave her pause. What hung unspoken between them was the fact that she carried his child. The least she could do would be to promise to be careful.

She sighed. "I'll tell the others about what happened and repeat your concerns."

"Thank you." He lifted a hand as if wanting to touch her, but seemed to stop himself and lowered his hand back to his side. "I need to go help Justin and Carlos check the rest of the vehicles. The last thing we want is a tractor tank full of diesel leaking all over the equipment barn."

Appreciation for his willingness to help softened her. "Call us if you need more sets of hands. Wait, I think I stuck my phone back in the bag, but I should check just in case . . ."

He handed over the plastic grocery bag, and she fished around until her fingers closed on her cell phone.

"Got it."

"You didn't block or delete my number, did you?" The hurt from being ghosted was clear in his voice.

The nasty taste of guilt was back. She hadn't had a choice, though. Even before she'd discovered she was pregnant, she'd known he had the power to hurt her. Because she'd liked him. Really, really liked him.

She couldn't cop to the truth, so she faked a bright smile. "Nope. Just ignored you."

He pulled in a noisy breath and readjusted his hat. "Heard. But promise you won't ignore my texts or calls now. I'll worry something has happened—"

"I promise, Alec. But everything will be fine." When in doubt, go for false bravado. Especially if it kept him from hovering over her. "Have you always been such a worrywart?"

He scoffed. "Hardly. Just the opposite, actually. As the baby of the family, I had plenty of people worrying over me and anything else that needed to be worried about. This is a new experience for me."

The reminder of how different their lives had been couldn't have been clearer. He came from wealth and privilege, delivered by a family who loved him dearly. She'd had to scrape for everything, living with the constant threat of being kicked to the curb.

She turned toward the back door. "Gotcha. Again, let us know if you need help."

She reached for the doorhandle, but he snagged her elbow and pulled her toward him. When she looked up at his face, he kissed her. Hard and quick with a blinding flash of passion.

Then he was gone, striding down the path and out of the main house's gated backyard.

Sammie's traitorous heart soared as she watched him go.

DESPITE THE RAPIDLY deepening gloom now that the sun had fully set, Alec lengthened his strides as he made his way toward the two bobbing beams of light emitted by Carlos's and Justin's flashlights. They were heading toward the equipment barn and could probably use his help checking all the different vehicles needed to run a large Texas ranch.

Alec would check everything from the largest combine to the smallest wheelbarrow to keep his mind off what he'd done tonight.

He'd kissed Sammie. Twice.

A jumble of worry, yearning, and foreboding kicked off a dustup in his gut. Alec wanted nothing more than for Sammie to be comfortable having him in her and their child's life. He couldn't afford to make her skittish. Especially if someone out there wished her and her friends ill.

Worry soundly won the battle of his belly as Alec entered the equipment barn. The large space was brightly lit by overhead lights that had been turned on by the other two men. Justin was dropping to the ground and working his way beneath the chassis of a green tractor. Carlos was on one knee, shining his flashlight beneath an ATV. Alec strode toward Justin, now only visible from the waist down.

Squatting, Alec peered beneath the tractor and watched as Justin aimed this flashlight's beam at the tractor's undercarriage. "Anything?" he asked.

"Nothing so far."

"Good. Good." Maybe there wasn't some sort of conspiracy against the women of Grit and Grace, or any lone bad actor wishing them ill. Alec chewed on the situation for a moment, then asked, "Could it have been a freak accident?" The *it* being a screwdriver to the gas tank of the truck Sammie had been driving.

Justin let out a heavy sigh as he pushed his way out from under the tractor. He sat up and propped his forearms on his bent knees. "You know, I've seen some crazy things happen on ranches. I once found a thousand-pound longhorn cow stuck upside down in a ditch that was barely two feet wide.

Wedged tight, all four legs sticking straight up. Her horns kept her head out, which was good, because I doubt we would have been able to pull her from the ditch otherwise. To this day I don't know for sure how she managed to get herself in that position, though I can think of a few possibilities. But I'm having a hard time picturing how that screwdriver punched into that gas tank at the angle I found it." He shrugged. "Like I said, I've seen some crazy things happen on ranches."

Alec nodded and extended a hand. Justin took it and Alec hoisted him to his feet.

Glancing at Carlos, Alec had to ask, "And the guys you have working here?"

Justin gave him a hard look. "Solid. I can personally vouch for every one. Asher will vouch for me if need be. We all came from the Hallidays' family ranch outside Houston, where Peyton, your soon-to-be sister-in-law, grew up. Hell, we all grew up there."

"And no one has a problem with women running the show?" Alec hated asking the question, but he had to cover all the bases.

"You have met Peyton, right? Seeing as she was the only Halliday with any real interest in that ranch, we were all happy to call her boss."

"Good enough. Had to ask."

"Understood."

Alec gestured toward another piece of farm machinery he

was very familiar with. "I'll take the baler."

Justin saluted him. "Much obliged."

As Alec made his way to the large red baler used to compress cut hay or other crops into cylinder-shaped rolls, Justin added, "Make sure there is nothing gumming up the belts."

"Will do," Alec said, having had the same thought. There were so many ways to make ranch work even more dangerous than it already was. A lesson he'd learned the hard way while growing up on the Wright Ranch. A decent night's sleep would be out of the question until he made certain the nagging worry tickling at the back of his neck was nothing more than a shadow from the past.

AFTER A DETOUR to her room with its ensuite bath, where she soaked a washcloth in cold water and held it to the back of her neck until she'd banked the fire Alec had started in her with nothing more than his kiss, Sammie grabbed her bag of snacks and joined the other women in the media room. Dressed in variations of loungewear and sprawled out on the overstuffed recliners arranged in theater-style seating, they were watching video clips of bulls and broncs Meira had compiled and was streaming from her laptop to the giant flat-screen TV mounted on the far wall. As each animal bucked its way across the screen, Meira filled them in on the bull's or bronc's pedigree and breeding potential. Laura would then interject how much acquiring the animal would set Grit and Grace back financially. The overall budget was not looking good.

With the weight of the unsecured Last Stand Rodeo roughstock contract heavy on her shoulders, Sammie plopped down in an empty recliner and started rummaging around in the bag of snacks. She'd tell them they had to add the cost of a new gas tank for the ranch truck after she had a little chocolate therapy. In the chair next to her, Beth leaned close enough to see what Sammie had in her bag.

Letting out a noisy sigh, Beth stood, flipped her long black braid over her shoulder, and left the room. She returned moments later with a meticulously plated meatloaf sandwich and thrust it at Sammie.

Sammie had no choice but to take the plate, giving the sandwich the sniff test as subtly as she could to make sure her touchy innards wouldn't rebel. Her stomach growled loudly with appreciation instead.

Beth nodded smugly and returned to her seat. Her nurturing way might extend to every living thing, but she definitely gave off more attitude when it came to people.

Allowing herself a few huge bites of sandwich, Sammie mentally weighed how best to tell her partners about the screwdriver-punctured gas tank. One thing she was certain of, though, was the necessity of downplaying Alec's concern over the incident. Mainly because she or, more specifically, her pregnancy, was the cause for his concern. She wasn't ready to tell them she had a baby on board. Not yet.

She was over halfway through the sandwich before she realized they had stopped talking and were all looking at her.

"Wha?" Sammie mumbled round a mouthful.

Laura set aside the spreadsheet in her hand. "I asked if you were able to write up the bid. Did Alec show you how?"

The moist meatloaf and tender bread turned to sawdust in her mouth. "Um." She forced the bite down her throat as all the things Alec could show her how to do flashed through her mind. "No. I mean, not really. We were interrupted."

Four sets of eyebrows went up.

Sammie set the plate with the remaining sandwich on the wide arm of the recliner. "I don't know if Laura mentioned what I texted her, but I forgot to fill the truck with gas before I went to town, and on the way back, the thing ran out of gas. Alec gave me a ride back." And kissed her. She absently moved the remaining sandwich around the plate. "Justin and Carlos volunteered to go get the truck, but when they tried putting more gas in, the fuel just ran out the bottom."

Emma sat forward. "There's a hole in the tank?"

Beth looked to Laura. "Can we afford a new tank?"

"Or a new truck," Emma said.

Laura retrieved the spreadsheet she'd set aside.

Meira asked Sammie, "Did it rust out?"

Needing to get to the point, Sammie said, "Justin found a screwdriver imbedded in the tank. The gas leaked out around the handle."

Emma exclaimed, "What?"

Meira frowned. "How?"

Leave it to Meira to want the details. Sammie shrugged. "I probably ran over the screwdriver somewhere and it flipped up and wedged itself into the tank."

Emma cocked her head. "That sounds . . ."

"Weird," Meira supplied.

Sammie's heart rate picked up. What if the guys' concerns weren't unfounded?

"What do Alec and Justin think?" Laura asked.

"They are out checking the other vehicles on the ranch," Sammie admitted.

"So they're worried." Laura reached for her phone.

"More like being overly cautious."

Laura glanced up from the phone and sent Sammie a stern look. "There is nothing wrong with being cautious."

Sammie held up her hands in surrender and anxiously waited to see who Laura was calling.

Phone to her ear, barely a moment passed before Laura said, "Hey, Justin. Sammie just told us what happened with the ranch truck."

Sammie relaxed back in the recliner. It made sense that Laura would call Justin. He was the ranch manager, after all. Alec was . . . Sammie didn't know what Alec was supposed to be, other than yet another complication in Sammie's life that she didn't need.

Laura listened for a minute. "Isn't it good that you didn't find anything else out of the ordinary?" She listened again. "Why do you think he's still worried?"

Sammie's breath froze in her lungs. What if Alec hadn't kept his promise to her?

"Hmm," Laura mused into the phone. "Of course. Yeah, we will." She ended the call.

"Well?" Emma asked.

"They don't know how or why the screwdriver ended up in the gas tank, but Alec is adamant we keep an eye out and be careful."

"Of?" Meira pressed.

Laura shrugged and set her phone aside. "Apparently, something happened on the Wright Ranch once, involving a ranch hand of theirs, or something. Left a mark on Alec, I guess."

Sammie frowned, trying to remember specifics from when she'd Googled the Neissons after Peyton learned Alec's brother Drew would be dogging her heels for the duration of the Pineville rodeo. Sammie remembered Peyton stopping her before she delved too deeply into the family lore. Clearly, it was past time to fill in the blanks as much as she could. She started hunting for her cell phone.

Meira had beaten Sammie to Google. "It says here that rodeo roughstock legend Thomas Wright and his extended family suffered a tragedy when a disgruntled former ranch hand released the Wright Ranch's prized bull into a paddock occupied by Thomas Wright's daughter and granddaughter. The granddaughter, Caitlin Neisson, escaped, but the daughter, Rebecca Neisson, mother of five and sole child of Thomas Wright, was trampled by the bull." Meira looked up, stricken. "She eventually died, ten years later, from her injuries."

"Oh no," Beth whispered.

Empathy sliced through Sammie's heart. No wonder Alec's family was so close. They'd been bonded by tragedy.

Meira continued reading aloud. "After Rebecca Neisson passed away, the ranch hand, Karl Fletcher, returned to Pineville and made several attempts on Caitlin Neisson's life but was apprehended."

Emma whistled through her teeth. "That poor family. No wonder Alec is paranoid."

Stunned, Sammie slumped deep into the recliner. She knew so little about Alec. The father of her child. The need to rectify the lack burned in her chest.

Almost as much as her heart ached for Alec.

Chapter Nine

AS THE HOUR passed nine p.m., the media room in the A Bar H Ranch's main house was silent as the women of Grit and Grace processed the results of their internet search. Spooked by what they'd learned about Alec's family's past and the unexplained screwdriver-punctured gas tank, the women decided to wrap up the virtual bull-and-bronc shopping session.

Beth stood. "I don't know about y'all, but I won't be able to sleep unless I check on the stabled animals."

"Agreed," Meira said as she set aside her laptop. She pushed herself to her feet. "I'll join you."

"Thanks. I'd probably freak myself out if I went in with the bulls by myself after hearing what happened to Alec's mom."

Laura stood also, gathering up her spreadsheets. "I don't think we really have anything to worry about in that regard. Peyton trusts Justin and Carlos, which is good enough for me. But it's never a bad idea to have a buddy when we're around the stock. Let's make that a rule going forward, shall we?"

The other ladies nodded their assent.

Laura continued, "Does anyone have anything else to share before we leave?" She looked pointedly at Sammie.

Sammie's cheeks heated with embarrassment and guilt for not correcting Laura's assumption that Sammie had secured the roughstock contract when they'd texted earlier. Studiously avoiding Laura's gaze, she grabbed the plate with the partially eaten sandwich, her bag of unhealthy snacks, and stood. She'd fess up first thing tomorrow morning.

She needed time to muster her courage. To figure out the best way to spin the truth so as not to upset her partners to the point she jeopardized her place here.

Sammie also needed time to find a way to deal with the emotions stirred up by learning what Alec had gone through. The grief for his childhood trauma. The sympathy for his loss of something she had never even known.

Emma, who was already heading out of the media room, called over her shoulder, "I'm going to check my truck. Took me three years to save up to buy that sucker. Anyone know where the flashlights are?"

"Yes," Meira shouted after Emma. "Be careful."

"There's one on the mudroom wall," Beth said over Meira.

Meira looked at Beth. "It's hiding in plain sight."

Beth grinned. "She'll never find it."

Laura gestured to the door. "Go show her."

As much as she'd like to help Emma, too, or find Alec and give him a massive hug, Sammie was hit by a wave of exhaustion. She doubted she could stay awake much longer. Carrying her plastic bag of junk food from the market and the dinner plate, she followed Beth and Meira out of the room.

Sammie had only taken a couple of steps down the hall on her way to the kitchen to dispose of her leftovers when a hand on her elbow stopped her.

"Wait up a sec," Laura said. When Sammie stopped, she released her arm. "Why didn't you tell the others about the contract? I almost told them earlier, but I didn't want to steal your thunder. Scoring our very first contract is your win, so you should be the one to crow about it."

Sammie flushed with shame. She should have told Laura the truth sooner. Now she couldn't bring herself to completely extinguish the flame of excitement that had turned Laura's hazel eyes to topaz in the dim light from the hall's wall sconces.

So she hedged. "I don't want to say anything yet because, well, it's not a done deal."

As Sammie had feared would happen, Laura's face fell. "It's not—?"

"I'm close," Sammie rushed to reassure Laura. "We're close. We're close to being given the contract."

Laura eyed Sammie, her skepticism clear.

Panic made Sammie's heart pound. Her friendship with

Laura might suffer because Sammie had misled her. The possibility made her break out in a sweat.

She quickly apologized. "I'm so sorry I made you think we already had the contract. That it was a done deal. But I'm working on it. I swear. Please don't be mad."

Laura pulled in a noisy breath, then released it slowly. "If Grit and Grace has any chance of succeeding, we have to be honest with each other, Sammie. Completely honest. I can't make sound financial decisions for us unless I have all the facts and information."

"You are right. You are so right." Her eyes burning with the threat of tears, Sammie stared down at the half-eaten sandwich on the plate she held. "And you have every right to be mad at me."

Laura gently reached for the plate, easing it from Sammie's white-knuckled grip. "I'm not mad, Sammie. But I am hurt. I want us to be able to trust each other. It's important for us to trust each other."

Sammie nodded mutely as all the secrets she wasn't trusting her friends with clamored around in her brain. Considering she was keeping a humungous secret—that she was pregnant with Alec Neisson's child—a fact she was nowhere near being ready to share yet because she hadn't quite wrapped her brain around it, she couldn't bear the burden of additional secrets.

Pulling in a steadying breath, Sammie said, "I hear you. And you're right. You absolutely should know what's going on." She squared her shoulders. "So, you already know I couldn't get a formal meeting with the Last Stand Rodeo officials and had to pretty much crash whatever they were doing at the saloon tonight, right?"

"Right." Laura was clearly reserving judgement.

"Well, what they were doing there at the saloon was meeting with Alec Neisson, who was acting as a representative of the Wright Ranch and is apparently going after the roughstock contract for next year's Last Stand Rodeo, as well."

Laura's eyes went wide. "What!? You're kidding."

Fearing they'd be overheard, Sammie glanced down the hall toward the kitchen, but the others appeared to have left the house already. She lowered her voice just in case. "Wish I was."

"Why would the Wright Ranch send us stock, then turn around and compete with us for what is now our hometown rodeo?"

"No idea." Alec's excuse about giving them a level playing field had to be just that, an excuse. Or his grandfather didn't consider Grit and Grace to be competition at all.

Holding Sammie's dinner plate in one hand, Laura tapped the side of her leg with her spreadsheets held in the other, clearly rolling possible answers around in her head. "And here I'd been thinking Alec came to Texas because of you."

Sammie blinked at her in surprise. While Laura hadn't

been thinking about Thomas Wright's motivations, she had recognized there was something between Sammie and Alec.

Granted, Sammie hadn't made a secret of spending the night with Alec in Pineville, but she'd worked hard at dismissing its importance. Because their one-night stand had been important. To the point it had scared her spitless.

For the first time in her life, Sammie had felt, if not cherished, then at least cared for. He had made her feel special, not like an object meant only to build himself up in some way. She'd had no idea what to make of those feelings. So she'd run, ignoring his attempts to contact her.

Wanting Laura's focus off whatever might be going on between her and Alec, Sammie steered the conversation back to the rodeo contract. "The rodeo officials were really complimentary towards us, though, and they had questions for Alec that he didn't have immediate answers for. When he called his brother to get the answers, he checked to see which animals they are sending us. Apparently, they are quality bulls and broncs. Alec also promised that not only will he show me how to write up a proper bid, but he'll make sure I get another opportunity to present it. I think we still have a chance, Laura. I really do."

One of Laura's brunette brows lifted, clearly not sold on their chances. There wasn't much more Sammie could do to convince her at the moment, but she did want to avoid having this conversation with the others. At least until she had something better to tell them.

Sammie worried the handles of the plastic bag with both hands in front of her. "I heard what you said about being honest with each other. I did. But do you think you can wait to tell the others all this until I can get our bid in front of the officials?"

Laura pursed her lips for a moment, then sighed. "Okay. For now. Because I know how important being able to fulfill this role for Grit and Grace is to you."

Sammie's throat closed tight over actually being seen by Laura. She managed to whisper, "Thank you."

Lifting the plate slightly, Laura asked, "You done with this?"

Sammie could only nod.

Laura smiled kindly. "Get some sleep, Sammie. You look like you could use it." She turned and walked to the kitchen.

Chased by a long-held fear that her grandmother was right about her, Sammie headed straight to her room. If she was actually seen by Laura, how much longer would it be before Laura—and the others—found her not worthy?

SAFE BEHIND THE locked door of the room that already felt like home, Sammie slumped against the dark-stained wood. Far too many emotions fought for dominance inside of her. Fear of being outed as a fraud. Insecurity about the strength of her welcome amongst women she truly cared for in a world she absolutely loved.

And probably strongest of all, a fierce protectiveness that was foreign to her. While explaining herself to Laura, she could have easily thrown Alec under the bus, made him out as the bad guy and to be blamed for her failure. But she hadn't. She'd done just the opposite.

She slid down the heavy bedroom door until she was sitting on the tiled floor that ran through the majority of the main house, the plastic bag of junk food on the floor next to her. The tile's coolness seeped through her jeans, grounding her, but doing little to dampen the heat of realization.

Sammie groaned aloud and pushed herself up off the floor. She made her way to the desk chair upholstered in a southwestern-style red fabric that matched the earth-toned diamond and bar shapes on the bedspread, then plunked down and started pulling her good cowboy boots off.

Why hadn't she taken the easy way out and placed the blame for missing the opportunity to land the rodeo contract squarely where it belonged, on Alec Neisson's broad shoulders? As the representative of who she now knew to be their biggest competitor, Alec could have served as a common enemy for the women of Grit and Grace.

Only he wasn't her enemy.

He was the father of her child.

A man who she couldn't just cut out of her life. Not now. And who knew what was driving him? While Sammie was driven by a need to prove her grandmother wrong, Alec might be driven by the need to prove his grandfather right, that trusting Alec to do a job had been the correct choice.

Sammie dropped her boots to the floor with a loud clatter and stood. Yanking her logoed shirt over her head without bothering to unbutton it, she tossed it at the laundry hamper in the corner, not caring if the shirt hit the mark. She made her way into the ensuite bathroom where she stripped off the rest of her clothing, donned her sleep shirt emblazoned with the words *Hot Blooded*, and prepared for bed.

She left the bathroom and mindlessly grabbed the bag of snacks off the floor and carried it to bed with her, despite having just brushed her teeth. Propped up by a mound of pillows, Sammie tore open the bag of dill pickle-flavored potato chips and started eating as she rolled Alec's importance to her around in her mind.

The fierce protectiveness burning in her chest wasn't only for the baby she carried. The feeling extended to Alec, for better or worse.

Because Alec was the father of her child. And the only man to have ever made her yearn for something she really hadn't thought she would ever have.

A family of her own.

A yearning she would do her darnedest to suppress.

ALEC WOKE LATE the next morning, having spent most of the night tossing and turning, imagining all the ways someone could wreak havoc on the A Bar H. Picturing all the ways Sammie could be placed in danger.

And remembering.

A swell of grief washed over him.

His mom in the hospital bed in a converted room in their house. His father silently weeping at her side. His sister's guilt for surviving.

Eventually, he'd fallen sound asleep right before dawn, which led to him oversleeping. Having grown up on a large working rodeo roughstock ranch, Alec had never needed an alarm clock. His days had always started at or before dawn. The bright morning sunlight shining through his room's window told him as clearly as the clock on his phone that he'd missed his usual wake-up time by a mile. He rushed to get dressed.

Alec walked out into the empty communal living area of the bunkhouse as he pulled a red-plaid cotton shirt over his white T-shirt and discovered that everyone else was long gone. He started to rethink the value of setting an alarm.

Especially now that he had a baby on the way. Not to mention the fact that his baby momma was stubborn and headstrong. As well as capable of disturbing his sleep all on her lonesome.

Alec wasn't here at the A Bar H on vacation, though. Recuperating a bad shoulder, yes, but seeing as there was nothing wrong with his head or other appendages, he needed to get a move on. There was always work to be done on a ranch and rarely enough hands to do it.

He stepped out of the bunkhouse into the bright July morning sun reflecting off the windshield of Justin's truck, parked near the door. Alec heard Justin speaking to someone before he saw them.

"Sure, you can borrow my rig. But like I said, I'd be more than happy to drive you."

"I know you're busy, so I don't want to inconvenience you more than I have to."

Sammie. Just the sound of her voice was enough to get Alec's heart pumping like straight shots of caffeine.

He rounded the hood of Justine's tan dually truck and found the tall ranch manager dangling a set of keys over the extended palm of the blonde beauty Alec found himself thinking of as his. She was wearing her town hat and boots again, with a light-washed version of the sparkly jeans she'd had on last night topped with a crisp, clean, white cotton button-down shirt. He strode toward the pair and slipped his palm over Sammie's.

"I got her, Justin. Thanks, man."

Sammie had reflexively wrapped her fingers around his hand before she reacted. "Wait, what? No. I need to get to town."

"And I'll take you in my truck. No worries." He used their joined hands to draw her toward his truck, parked alongside Justin's.

"That's okay, I can drive myself—" Sammie made a grab for Justin's keys.

The other man met Alec's gaze, and clearly read Alec's intent to not let Sammie, or any of the women of Grit and Grace, be unaccompanied until they knew what was up. Justin closed the keys within his palm and lifted it just out of her reach.

Sammie's shoulders slumped and she gave Justin an *et tu, Brute?* look.

Justin shrugged, smiling apologetically, then tipped his hat to them both. "Take care, you two." He turned and sauntered off toward the bronc barn.

"No, I—Justin!" Sammie called after him, but he ignored her. Alec had already started tugging her around the hood of his new truck.

She tugged in the opposite direction. "Alec, I need to go to town."

He tossed her his best grin but didn't release her or give any ground. "And I'm more than happy to take you." He opened the passenger door of his truck and guided her toward the seat.

She braced herself in the opening. "I want to go by myself."

Alec froze. "Do you have a doctor appointment?"

She glanced around them, as if checking for anyone within hearing distance, then met his gaze directly. "No.

That's not why I'm going into town."

He held her gaze.

She glared back, then huffed out a breath. "I just need to get to town. You taking me or not?" she snapped.

"You know you're cute when you're annoyed."

"Just wait until you see me pissed."

He laughed. He really did like her.

She rolled her eyes and climbed into his truck.

"Be sure to buckle up," Alec reminded her cheerfully before swinging the passenger door shut on her dirty look.

Halfway expecting her to change her mind and bolt back out of his truck, Alec hustled around to the driver's side and climbed in. Luckily, his keys and wallet were still in the jeans he'd shucked off last night, then pulled right back on this morning after running late. He started the truck and headed them toward the ranch exit and the road to town.

They sat in a silence that could have been characterized as companionable if it weren't for Sammie continually wringing her hands in her lap. Alec tried to pretend he didn't notice, but he felt in the pit of his gut her upset, or nerves, or whatever it was that had her wound up like a bull in a chute with his flank strap pulled tight too soon.

Even though they were a good five miles outside of town, he asked, "So where to, boss?"

She kept her gaze trained out the front windshield. "Um, you can just drop me off in front of the saloon."

He slanted her a glance. "I'm pretty sure it's not open

yet."

"I know. But it'll let me walk . . . you know, um, around town."

Alec began to suspect Sammie might have her first prenatal doctor appointment. He was not willing to miss attending it with her, so he said brightly, "Great. I'll come with. I've been wanting to check out Last Stand. I've heard the place has a lot of history, going clear back to the late 1800s. Have you seen that statue in the town square yet? I heard it's modeled after the guy who saved everyone in the saloon—"

She heaved a sigh. "I'm going to the rodeo grounds."

"Ah," he said, as understanding dawned. "Pre-rodeo set up. A good time to *bump into* the officials, chat about next year's rodeo."

Her shoulders raised nearly to her ears, she gripped her thighs and focused her attention out the side window.

Something shifted in Alec's chest. He softened his tone. "Did you get a chance to fill out that bid form I sent you?"

"Not yet."

"I can help you. If you'd like."

She looked at him, her gaze wary and full of suspicion. "Why?"

"Why? Why would I help you? You seriously have to ask that?"

"Yes, Alec, I do. Considering I interrupted your meeting with the people I need to meet with but couldn't get a meeting with!"

She had a point. Alec twisted his hands on the steering wheel. He decided to go with the truth. "I'll help you because I want to. I want you to succeed, Sammie. And not just because you are pregnant with our child."

"But you can't let down your grandfather, Alec."

She hadn't said it as a question, but as a leaden weight settled deep in his belly, he answered, "No. I can't."

Chapter Ten

A HEAVY SILENCE sat between Alec and Sammie as he drove his new black truck through town toward the rodeo grounds, the bright morning sun already shining hot into the cab. While Sammie's attention appeared to be intent on the businesses they passed, he doubted she was really seeing the Char-Pie Bakery, Hutchinson's BBQ Market, or the People's Bank of Last Stand with its neighboring garden. He doubted Main Street was making much of an impression on her. Her grip on her thighs had remained tight.

As determined as he was to stick close to her, at least until they had a reasonable answer for how that screwdriver ended up buried in the gas tank of the truck she'd been driving, he also didn't want to cause her undue stress. She was already dealing with more than her share.

An unplanned pregnancy being first and foremost.

Alec was concerned for her. And their child.

On top of her relatively new condition, she was trying to help start a rodeo roughstock business in a very competitive environment. Guilt pinched him. Sammie had been right when she'd said he couldn't let his grandfather down. He had to prove himself. But even without his, and thus the Wright Ranch's, presence here in Last Stand, there were plenty of others in the area who could provide the rodeo with rough stock.

In addition, there might—and he would stress the *might* until he knew for sure—be someone who didn't want women as competition.

While the guilt invading his chest made him want to back off and give her the space she might need to cope with the stress from the added competition he'd brought with him, his worry for her safety demanded he stick close to her.

There was no way he could back off. Like it or not, she was now a part of his family, and he would always protect family.

THE ENTIRE DRIVE through town, Sammie was aware of Alec glancing at her, but luckily, he didn't press her into conversation. She'd needed the time to come up with a game plan.

The best she could come up with was to ditch Alec.

Somehow.

Then find and court the rodeo officials so she could give them the envelope containing the bid she'd written up, using Alec's template, currently folded in half and tucked into her back pocket and hopefully out of sight.

Somehow.

As difficult as those tasks might seem, the one that really worried her was her ability to remain unaffected by the man seated next to her in the big truck. She had to find a way to separate Grit and Grace from her personal situation.

Her situation. Such a nice euphemism.

"What's so funny?" Alec asked.

Only then did Sammie realize she was smiling.

"Nothing. I was just thinking about something Emma said," she lied.

"Oh?" He turned into the rodeo grounds parking area, clearly expecting her to share.

She gave him her sweetest, fakest smile. "Just girl stuff."

He opened his mouth to say something, then shut it, clearly thinking better of commenting. Smart man.

"There's a spot." She pointed at an available parking space in the surprisingly full lot.

Alec pulled past the space, then put the truck in reverse and effortlessly backed into the spot. Perfectly. Sammie would expect no less from a born and bred cowboy.

She didn't give him a chance to be chivalrous and help her out of the truck. She opened the passenger door and jumped out all by her lonesome.

And promptly almost puked. Whether it was the smell from this year's rough stock being brought in by the trailer-full or the sudden motion of jumping out of Alec's truck. She grabbed her hair up in one hand, bent forward, and braced her other hand on her knee, breathing through the wave of nausea.

Alec's hand settled gently on her back, rubbing little circles. He didn't say a word, just waited patiently for her to either hurl or get on with it. Thankfully, the hard-boiled egg and toast she'd eaten before leaving the main house stayed put.

Sammie straightened, blowing like a bronc after a bucking battle. Alec kept a gentle but steadying hand on her. As soon as she was certain she wasn't about to decorate her good boots, she turned to face him. He dropped his hand to his side.

The empathy and concern on his handsome face made her heart skip a beat. Why did he have to be so amazing? The hurt would be exponentially worse when he left her.

He raised his blond brows in silent question.

"I'm good. Really. I'm good."

He raised his hand again as if intending to touch her, but instead hooked his thumb in the front pocket of his jeans. "Promise you'll let me know if there's anything I can do."

Okay, make yourself scarce.

"I will. Thanks," she said instead.

"Ready?"

Sammie fluffed out her hair and straightened her shoulders. "Yes."

Alec grinned. "Attagirl." He stepped aside to let her lead the way to the entrance of the rodeo arena.

Alec's long stride brought him even with her as they passed through the unmanned admission booths and the concessions area, where various food vendors were setting up their trucks and signage. Luckily, nothing was being deep fried or roasted or made smelly in any way. The nausea stayed at bay.

They weaved their way through the hive of activity toward the rodeo arena. Banners for advertisers, from the giant national ranch equipment manufacturers to the small local feed store, were hung on every available space on the backside of the wooden stadium seats and on the sides of the tunnel-like walkway they took to the arena.

When she and Alec stepped out of the tunnel, they paused to take in the organized chaos inside the large oval arena, ringed by metal pole fencing also adorned with advertisers' banners. Some of the rodeo's competitors were familiarizing themselves, and their horses, with the arena and the chutes before the slack rounds, comprised of the overflow competitors, slated to start the next day.

Sammie spotted a group of older men standing smack dab in the middle of the arena, seemingly oblivious to the riders. She recognized them as the men who had gathered at the saloon to hear Alec's pitch.

If she tried to approach them now, with Alec by her side, she didn't doubt for a moment that they would want to speak with him, seeking answers to whatever questions he hadn't been able to answer the other night.

It was time to ditch Mr. Amazing. And she knew just how to do it.

"Alec?" She turned to him and started fiddling with a lock of hair. A cheap tactic, she knew, but if it worked, it worked.

His gaze jumped from the curl she'd wrapped around a finger to her mouth, to her eyes. "Yeah?"

Forcing herself to ignore the tingle of awareness his interest had started in her lips and other places, she said, "You know how you wanted me to promise to tell you if I needed anything?"

He straightened. "What can I do for you?"

His earnestness gave her pause.

She pushed it aside. All was fair in love and rodeo.

"I suddenly have a craving. A huge craving."

His eyes flared with curiosity. "What do you need?"

It was a struggle to keep from smiling. "A corn dog."

He blinked. "A corn dog? It's not even nine a.m."

"I know it's weird, but . . ." She gestured to her still-flat belly.

Understanding dawning across his handsome face, he held up a hand. "I gotcha. Is one enough?"

She couldn't contain her smile any longer. "Yeah, one is enough."

With a quick tug on the brim of his cowboy hat, he turned on his bootheel and headed back toward the concourse area where the food vendors were setting up. No way would he find one even close to being able to produce the deep fried bliss on a stick. Not this early in the day. She'd bought herself at least a little time.

With her pulse picking up its pace, Sammie waited until Alec had disappeared back through the tunnel under the grandstands, then hurried toward the entrance gate into the arena. With a brief moment of regret for her pristine dress cowboy boots, she stepped into the deep, rich combination of sand, silt, and clay used to soften an impact for both human and animal competitors. Normally, Sammie loved the smell of a rodeo arena, but today she concentrated on breathing through her mouth.

Dodging the equestrian team practicing one of their between-events routines, their pole-mounted American and Texas state flags flapping and snapping noisily in the quickly heating morning air, Sammie hurried as best she could through the six inches of loose dirt toward the circle of older men and one woman holding a clipboard.

When Sammie reached the group, one of the men, a short, balding, middle-aged man with generous eyebrows she recognized from the saloon the evening before, was pointing toward the raised wood-and-metal announcer's stand above the chutes, saying, "Can someone please move the Outlaw Tequila banner to the left to center it? Can't have it looking like we've been sampling our sponsors goods *too* much."

The other men chuckled and elbowed each other. The woman with the clipboard noticed Sammie first.

"Can I help you?"

Sammie plastered on her biggest smile and extended her hand to the woman. "Hi, I'm Sammie Abel, of Grit and Grace Rodeo Roughstock Company."

"Ah yes, the persistent Ms. Abel." The woman shifted her clipboard and took Sammie's hand and gave it a quick courtesy shake. "Regina Rhinehart, Rodeo Secretary."

The grand pooh-bah of the Last Stand Rodeo. Sammie resisted the urge to curtsey.

The man who had been pointing noticed Sammie and he smiled broadly. "Look who's here! Grit and Grace."

Sammie stepped forward and offered her hand to him. "Sammie Abel."

"Gene Bauer, Arena Director."

They had the attention of the other men, so Gene gestured to them. "This is Skip Hinds, our Operations Manager, and that's Mark Cantor, Marketing Coordinator."

Sammie greeted and shook hands with the other men. "Pleased to meet you." She turned back to Gene. "I'm so sorry I interrupted your meeting with Alec Neisson—"

Gene looked past her, and his round face lit up. "And speak of the devil."

"My ears are ringing. What'd I miss?"

Sammie whirled around and found Alec grinning down at her.

"As requested, one corn dog for the pretty lady." Alec held up a perfectly browned battered hot dog on a stick wrapped in a napkin. Steam rose from the obviously freshly made dog.

Glancing between the food and his blue eyes, bright with a distinct *gotcha* gleam, Sammie blurted, "How—?"

Alec shrugged. "I have my ways."

He did indeed.

Alec offered Sammie the corn dog, and she had no choice but to take it. Her treacherous stomach growled in appreciation.

"Oh, and here." Alec dug in his shirt pocket, producing packets of mustard and ketchup. "I didn't know which you liked so I grabbed both."

The glint of triumph was gone from his gaze, replaced by the awareness of how little they knew about each other.

Sammie took the offered condiment packets, her fingers lingering on his. He really was amazing. And she was in deep trouble.

Gene moved past her so he could place a friendly hand on Alec's shoulder. "Now about those questions we had for your—"

Just like that, Sammie saw her chance slipping away.

Again.

"Excuse me, Mr. Bauer, but I'd like to submit a bid . . ." She struggled to pull the folded envelope from her back pocket without dropping the mustard and ketchup packets. Alec shifted and reached toward her as if to help. She shot him a warning look and finally managed to produce the envelope. She extended it to Bauer. "Please accept Grit and Grace Rodeo Roughstock Company's bid for next year's rodeo."

Gene Bauer eyed the envelope, but didn't take it. He considered her a moment. "I'll tell you what, Miss Abel." He gave Alec's shoulder a squeeze and pat before releasing him. "We just discovered the trick riding and roping act we'd contracted to perform an exhibition at this year's rodeo has canceled on us."

Skip, the operations manager, interjected, "Appendicitis."

Alec asked, "Rider or horse?"

The men looked at each other as if the question hadn't occurred to them. Sammie glared at Alec, then glowered when he winked at her.

Regina sighed. "Rider."

Gene waved the nonsense off. "As I was saying, we find ourselves down one act."

The marketing guy said, "An act we advertised extensively."

Gene nodded. "Indeed. We'd like to replace that exhibition with something of equal or greater appeal."

The corn dog lost its appeal as Sammie started to glean where Gene was heading. "I'm so sorry to hear about the cancellation, but what—?"

He pointed at the envelope. "Tell ya what. I'll take a look at your bid for next year—"

A spurt of elation made Sammie dizzy.

"—if you and your fellow Buckin' Babes agree to put on an exhibition of gals giving broncs what for during this year's rodeo."

Sammie's euphoria was snuffed in the dirt faster than a bull rider with greased britches. She lowered the envelope.

"She can't ride," Alec said with a thunderous frown.

Gene's bushy brows went up. "Oh?"

Sammie pointed the corn dog at Alec in warning not to say another word, then tried to make the threat appear to be a more casual gesture. "What he means is that I can't ride without first clearing the exhibition with my partners. But just so you know, the five of us have retired from the ranch bronc riding circuit. We are rodeo roughstock ranchers now. Thus . . . this." She waved the envelope.

Gene dismissed her with an, "Oh, *pish*. It's not like you'll be competing. You'll just be giving the local folks here a taste of celebrity. That show you gals were on was very popular in these parts. A lot of people would enjoy seeing you do your thing in real life."

Alec made a noise at Gene's reference to *real life*.

Regina's expertly sculpted brows were high as she looked between the men.

Alec shifted his weight to one leg and hooked his thumbs in his front pockets. "What about me?"

Gene's brows came together into one bushy fringe. "What about you?"

"Got to say, I'm a little hurt you didn't ask me to climb on a bull this year in order to submit a bid for next year."

Gene pulled his chin in. "Do you want to?"

Alec's injured shoulder twitched upward. "Not particularly. But my point is, I don't have to do anything in exchange for the opportunity to have my bid considered."

Scoffing, Skip said, "Of course not. Thomas Wright—"

"Already has a respected reputation in rodeo," Gene cut the older man off.

"Trust me," Alec said, his tone ominous. "My grandfather acquired that reputation because he has never traded a performance of any kind for the chance to bid a rodeo."

Afraid Alec was on the brink of sinking both of their chances, Sammie interrupted. "No, it's okay. Really. I will hustle back to the A Bar H and see what my partners have to say. I already know Emma will be game."

Mark, the marketing guy, said, "Is she the little pistol who rode for the investors you had out? I hear she put on a good show."

Sammie gripped the condiment packets so tightly one of them started to leak in her hand. Willie Bite put on the show. Emma simply knew when and how to get off the big bronc.

Plastering on a toothy smile, Sammie said, "That's our Emma."

Gene clapped his hands together. "Wonderful. If you, Miss Abel, could get back to us, and by us, I of course mean

Regina, by the end of today, it'd be much appreciated." He shifted his attention to Alec. "And you need to get back to me."

Still looking stepped on, Alec nevertheless said, "Yes, sir."

Gene nodded. "Now I have a banner that needs moving, so if you'll excuse us?"

Alec reached for Sammie's elbow and gently drew her away.

Sammie called out to the group, "Thank you for your time!" Admittedly, she sounded pitiful.

With her elbow in Alec's grip, Sammie allowed him to lead her from the arena. Her good boots were like concrete blocks she was having to drag through the deep dirt.

Alec didn't rush her. It took everything in her not to lean into him for support. He'd already supported her by sticking up for her in a way she would have never imagined. As he guided her through the arena entrance, shielding her from the tons of horseflesh galloping by as the equestrian team practiced their entrance, Sammie considered his handsome profile. The man was downright beautiful. On the inside as well as outside.

Hopefully, their baby took after his or her daddy. Her chest warmed as the reality of her condition struck her anew. She was having Alec Neisson's child. Thomas Wright's great-grandchild.

She just might hurl after all.

"You didn't really want that corn dog, did you?" Alec

asked as they moved clear of the arena and headed to the parking lot.

Sammie looked at what she'd forgotten she held. Blessedly, the deep fried snack still smelled good to her. "Actually, I did." She took a huge bite, the salty-savory-sweet combination hitting her tongue like heaven. "I just didn't think you'd be able to actually get one," she mumbled around the bite.

"Never forget, Miss Abel, I'm a man of many talents."

She arched an eyebrow at him. "Are you saying you made this?"

"If by made you mean I paid the vendor two hundred and forty dollars to fire up his fryer and whip up one corn dog, then yes."

Sammie nearly choked. "This is a two-hundred-and-forty-dollar corn dog?"

He grinned down at her. "Worth it if you like it."

"Alec!" she chastised him, but a tiny, secret part of her was thrilled by his generosity. The rest of her shouted that the fact he had that kind of money to throw away on a batter-coated tube of processed meat was reason enough for her to run for the hills.

They came from very different worlds. She couldn't forget that.

Wetness in the palm of her other hand caught her attention. She raised the hand still clutching the envelope with the bid she'd agonized over. She opened her fingers and stopped. Alec stopped as well. They both stared down at the bottom half of the envelope, stained red with ketchup from the packet she'd burst the seal on.

Without saying a word, Alec took the envelope, ketchup and mustard packets from her hand and eased out one of the napkins he'd wrapped around the corn dog stick to wipe the mess from Sammie's palm.

Her vision suddenly blurred with unshed tears. She met his gaze. "Thank you."

He leaned in and gave her a gentle, heartbreakingly sweet kiss.

Everything in her, especially her heart, was pulled to him just as the tide was pulled to the moon.

He started to ease the corn dog from her hand. Sammie snapped out of his thrall and tightened her grip.

"No! I want this."

A smile tugged at his sensual mouth. "Okay. Sorry."

When he folded the ketchup-gunked envelope and started to put it in his back pocket, she stopped him.

"Wait. I need that."

"You didn't save it on your computer?"

She had, but she didn't want to risk him opening it and seeing what a pathetic—or outrageous, she really didn't know—bid she'd committed to paper. Sure, he'd stuck up for her and her friends, but he didn't have to pay to play like they did. With his grandfather's name and reputation backing him, he'd never know what it was like to try to reach for the stars while on your back in a ditch.

When she got right down to what mattered to her, she didn't want Alec to think badly of her. And not just because she'd found herself pregnant with his child.

Her grandmother would be crowing from the rooftop.

With a shudder, Sammie admitted to herself she also didn't want to rob her friends of their choices. They had the right to know what price they'd have to pay to get their first rodeo roughstock contract.

They had the right to choose. As well as know that she hadn't been able to do the job they'd entrusted to her. Or why she couldn't participate if they decided to ride.

Chapter Eleven

ALEC HAD BARELY driven his truck out of the Last Stand Rodeo grounds parking area when Sammie, looking very much like she belonged in the passenger seat of his truck, stripped the last of the corn dog off its stick.

She eyed the stick thoughtfully. "Is it wrong that I'm still hungry?"

Alec grinned, turning the wheel toward town. "Not at all. Why do you think those things aren't a breakfast staple? Not filling at all."

She laughed, a light sound he hadn't realized he missed until he heard it again. "I'm afraid I opened the tap by eating this. I think I could eat a whole pig. Or cow. Or whatever these hot dogs were made of."

"Probably best not to know."

She licked the side of the stick and Alec's lower belly contracted. Phallic connotations aside, how could he be so attracted to her after watching her inhale a corn dog? For breakfast.

Because she was the most beautiful, smart, funny, and

courageous woman he'd ever met, that's why. And yeah, her eating a corn dog was hot.

He wasn't ready for her to bail from his truck the minute they returned to the ranch and shut him out again.

Keeping his eyes on the road, he asked, "How about a proper breakfast?"

"Proper? Like with sausages? Made of ground-up meat in casings like . . ."

"Hot dogs. Yes."

She grinned back at him. "Actually, French toast sounds really good right now."

"Pretty sure we can find some French toast." The tightness that had gripped his chest since Gene Bauer had made his outrageous stipulation to consider Sammie's bid eased slightly. At least there was something he could do for her right now. "When I was staying in town, a spot called Kolaches was recommended to me for breakfast, but I never made it there before I moved out to the ranch. Do you want to give it a try?"

She took her time wrapping the corn dog stick in the remaining napkin. Was she weighing the cost of spending time with him? Or was she thinking about having to tell the other women the cost of being able to submit a bid for the Last Stand Rodeo?

The tightness returned to Alec's chest. He was so angry, frustrated, and downright offended Gene was going to make the women, who he found himself no longer thinking of solely as the Buckin' Babes, give a ranch saddle bronc riding exhibition in exchange for the chance to submit a bid. Despite what Alec had promised her, the playing field was *not* level.

He could always refuse to submit his own bid from the Wright Ranch in protest, but doing so would cost him the one thing he truly needed—his grandfather's approval. He'd never be put in charge of the Wright Ranch bucking bull program without proving he could reliably accomplish tasks Thomas Wright gave him.

Besides, withholding the Wright Ranch bid probably wouldn't make a difference. There were enough ranches in the area around Last Stand that could supply their rodeo with the rough stock they needed. It would be an empty gesture.

Sammie closed her fingers around the napkin-wrapped stick and sighed. "Yes. Let's give it a try."

"Great."

He might not be able to level the playing field for her, but at least he could feed her. Admittedly, a self-serving offering. He really wanted to spend more time with the woman carrying his child. There was so much about Sammie he didn't know. He wanted, needed, to discover the inner workings of this intriguing woman. For his child's sake. And his own.

THE MOMENT THE heaping plate of biscuits and sausage gravy was placed in front of Alec, seated across from Sammie at a window table in Kolaches German bakery, he realized Sammie wasn't the only hungry one. Sammie made all sorts of appreciative noises after her plate of powdered sugar-coated French toast, an egg, and a small bowl of mixed fresh berries was set in front of her, along with a little ceramic pitcher of syrup.

Without a moment's hesitation, she used her fork to scoop the egg up and placed it on top of the French toast, dumped the entire bowl of berries atop the egg, then drowned it all in maple syrup.

Caught somewhere between shock and awe, Alec asked, "Is that how you usually . . . um . . ." He gestured with his fork at the sugar bomb she'd created on her plate.

She stared blankly at him for a beat, then caught his meaning. "Oh. I . . ." She considered her plate. "No, actually. Just seems like a good idea. At the moment." She glanced around them before leaning back and placing a hand on her lower stomach. "Because, you know."

Something flipped behind his sternum. She was pregnant with his child. While he didn't think it would be a problem, Alec needed Sammie's assurance that regardless of what her partners decided, she wouldn't ride anything besides the most docile pony.

Watching her destroy her breakfast with unbridled pleasure, he decided the conversation could wait until they had eaten.

He polished off his biscuits and gravy in the same amount of time it took Sammie to finish her French toast, egg, and fruit mash-up.

Alec sat back in his chair in satisfaction. As much as he wanted to simply enjoy this moment with Sammie, some things just needed to be said. "I'm sorry Gene Bauer wouldn't take your bid, Sammie."

She stopped pushing a fat blueberry through the pool of syrup on her plate. "He'll take it. Eventually."

"But only if you agree to the bronc riding exhibition."

She shrugged nonchalantly, as if the requirement didn't matter. But she slowly set her fork down, the blueberry abandoned.

He sat forward again, settling his forearms on either side of his empty plate. "Tell me you're not going to ride, Sammie."

She sat back, away from him, a thundercloud forming on her beautiful face. "Alec, even though this . . ." She pointed meaningfully down at her stomach. "Wasn't planned, I'd never, ever do anything to jeopardize . . ." She glanced around again. "Junior. Frankly, the fact that you think you have to remind me to be careful—"

Alec held up his hands to stop her before she really worked up a head of steam. "Okay, okay. I'm sorry. I trust you, Sammie. I do. But I guess I just needed to hear you say the words."

"Why, Alec? Why do you need to be reassured? You aren't the one having to pay to play."

Boy, he'd really stepped in it. "Because I can't do anything to help you."

"Can't you?"

He met her stormy-blue gaze. They both knew he could at least make the gesture. He could pack up his things and remove the Wright Ranch and his grandfather's reputation from the equation. But he wouldn't. Not only because doing so wouldn't matter. He had to prove himself to his grandfather. His future, the future of his child, and hopefully, one day Sammie, relied on him succeeding here in Last Stand.

He reached a hand across the table, palm up. "I'm sorry, Sammie."

She stared at his hand for a moment. Her chest rose as she breathed deeply, then she slid her hand over his, joining their palms. He felt the contact deep in his chest.

Her face softened. "It's okay, Alec. And I'm sorry, so very sorry, for what you had to go through."

He tucked his chin, confused. "For what I had to . . .?"

She covered their joined hands with her other one. "Your mom. I'm so sorry about what happened to your mom."

The sore spot he would always have on his heart flinched. "I was young."

She tightened her grip on his hand. "But you weren't when she finally passed."

"How—?" His voice caught.

"Last night when we were trying to figure out why you were so worried about the screwdriver, why you wanted all the vehicles checked, Meira—I'm sorry, it seems so invasive now—but Meira Googled your family and found out about the ranch hand—"

"Karl Fletcher." Just saying the name was like staring again into the black hole that had sucked so much joy from his life. It was also a reminder of how freely the internet divulged private matters for the world to see, uncaring of the wounds that were inflicted or, in his case, reopened. Keeping secrets was nearly impossible in this day and age.

Her blue eyes glistened with unshed tears. "Yes. Him. It explained a lot."

"It was a long time ago, Sammie."

"But I know what it's like to grow up without a mom. For completely different reasons, but still, I know it leaves a mark."

Realizing this was a chance for him to learn more about the mother of his child, Alec added his free hand on top of hers. "Tell me."

She glanced around them, clearly aware they were in a busy restaurant. "Another time." Apparently, she didn't want to rehash her past in public any more than he did.

He found himself scanning the restaurant also, on the lookout for phones aimed their way. If their secret, that she was carrying his child, got out before she agreed to let him tell his family . . . There would be hell to pay, for sure.

She eased her hand out from underneath his and sat back in her chair. "We'll figure it out."

He pulled his too-empty-feeling hands off the table. His brain knew she meant that she and her friends would figure out what to do about having to pay to play. The rest of him, though, wanted her to mean that the two of them would figure out how to come together. As parents. Maybe more.

Because he was falling for Sammie Abel.

Hard.

THE EXPECTATION AND barely contained excitement was a palpable thing in the A Bar H main house dining room as the partners of Grit and Grace worked together to get their dinner on the table. Luckily, Laura had been the only one present in the house when Alec had dropped Sammie off after their time at the rodeo setup and breakfast in town.

Laura, elbow deep in spreadsheets, had distractedly accepted Sammie's excuse for not revealing whether she'd successfully met with the rodeo officials until everyone was together.

While it was true Sammie only wanted to explain their dilemma once, she'd also been hit with a massive carb coma after the breakfast Alec had treated her to and she'd needed a nap. Or maybe it was a sugar crash. Maybe she'd hit an exhaustion wall because she'd stayed up too late filling in numbers pulled straight from thin air into the bid template Alec had emailed her. Whatever the cause for her exhaustion, immediately after speaking to Laura, Sammie had escaped to her room and her bed, sleeping until after lunch.

The frustration, anxiety, and her growing feelings toward Alec... all the feelings she'd been able to escape while she slept were back, amplified by the anticipation radiating from the other women in the kitchen and dining room. Sammie simply needed to stick with her plan of telling them what Gene Bauer wanted in exchange for a chance to bid on next year's rodeo and allow them to make their choice.

As had become their habit, Sammie laid out the table place settings, Emma made and brought out the sweet tea, Meira was in charge of the salad, while Laura and Beth produced the bulk of the evening meal. Except for pizza night. Sammie was awesome at ordering and picking up pizza.

Alec had offered to *pop in* at dinner time to provide Sammie with moral support when she told the other women what Gene had said, but despite the warmth his offer had ignited within her, she'd declined. This was her job to do, and she'd never be able to keep Grit and Grace separate from her personal life if she relied on him at every turn.

She couldn't stop herself from imagining, or at least attempting to imagine, what it would be like to rely on someone else. A man. Alec, specifically. She'd never had anyone to really look out for her. Someone who didn't criticize her at every turn. Someone who wanted the best for her, not out of selfishness, but because they loved her.

Sammie lingered at the sideboard, pretending to search for a slotted spoon for the steamed vegetables, until the food was all on the table and the four other women were taking their seats. Placing the spoon in the white casserole dish Laura had steamed the mixed veggies in, Sammie took her seat. Luckily, the smell of the veggies and the baked pork chops didn't set off her currently overactive gag reflex.

Not quite ready to drop the bomb Gene Bauer had stuck her with, Sammie asked no one in particular, "Any new screwdrivers found stuck where they don't belong?"

Meira shook her head. "Justin said they checked every vehicle and piece of equipment and found nothing, aside from an empty bird's nest in the old tractor and a batch of kittens in the backhoe's bucket."

"Kittens?!" Beth, the caretaker of all things furry and otherwise, pushed her chair back and started to get up.

Meira put out a staying hand. "Justin found the momma and made up a box for them. They'll be fine until after dinner."

Beth grumbled but regained her seat and scooted back up to the table.

Sammie accepted the plate of pork chops being passed around the table and chose one to add to her plate. "So, we're chalking up the screwdriver stuck in the truck gas tank as a freak accident?"

Laura said, "Lacking any reason not to, yes."

Relieved that at least something was going their way, Sammie added a helping of steamed vegetables to her plate. The salad was the only thing that didn't appeal to her tonight. "Good. Good. Any word from the investors?"

Laura tipped her head back and forth. "Yes, and no."

Emma asked, "Meaning?"

"They are interested but won't commit until we land our first contract. Speaking of which . . ." Laura, along with the three other women, looked to Sammie.

Showtime.

Sammie set down her knife and fork. "I was able to find the Last Stand Rodeo officials at the arena."

Emma all but bounced in her chair. "And? What did they say?"

Sammie adjusted the position of her knife until it was perfectly aligned with her spoon. "They will look at a bid from us."

Emma whooped while Laura and Meira high-fived.

Beth narrowed her eyes at Sammie. "But?"

Sammie let out a noisy breath. "But . . .they need an act, or something, to replace the trick riding exhibition that just canceled on them. They want us to perform a ranch saddle bronc riding exhibition at this year's rodeo. As the Buckin' Babes. Well, the former Buckin' Babes, that is. Then they will accept a bid from us."

Beth blinked. "This year's rodeo? As in the Fourth of

July rodeo happening at the end of this week?"

Meira asked, "Did you tell them we're retired?"

Sammie nodded. "I did. But Gene Bauer, the arena director, had heard about Emma's ride from at least one of the investors we'd invited out here to the A Bar H. Apparently, she was a little too entertaining. He's excited to see her and the rest of us ride too."

Emma screwed up her face. "Sorry?"

Laura grew thoughtful. "And he won't accept a bid from us for next year's rodeo roughstock contract unless we put on an exhibition this year?"

"Correct. I had the bid with me, but Gene wouldn't take it."

Emma said, "That's blackmail. They can't do that. Can they do that?"

Meira leaned forward toward Sammie. "Justin mentioned that Alec had driven you to the rodeo grounds. Was he there when this Gene person told you the conditions for accepting our bid?"

Sammie's gaze jumped to Laura's. The expression in her eyes was expectant. Clearly, she was waiting for Sammie to confess that Alec was bidding for the same contract. Just like her other secret, Sammie knew the truth about Alec acting as the Wright Ranch's representative would come out eventually. The truth always did. "Yes, he drove me. And he was standing right next to me when Gene laid out the deal."

Meira's reddish-brown brows arched. "Did he have anything to say about said deal?"

Sammie felt a smile tug at her mouth with the memory. "He asked if they expected him to climb on a bull in exchange for his bid."

Emma smirked. "Do they?"

Meira caught on quicker. "Wait, what? His *bid*?"

Sammie slumped back in her chair. "Alec is here in Last Stand to try to get next year's roughstock contract for the Wright Ranch."

"No," Beth breathed out.

Sammie could only shrug.

Everyone sat silently for a moment, digesting Sammie's words as their dinner grew cold on their plates.

Emma finally asked Sammie, "Do they?"

"Do they what?"

"Expect Alec to ride a bull in exchange for his bid?"

Sammie allowed a ghost of a smile at Emma's tenacity. "No."

Emma threw her napkin on her plate. "See! They can demand we ride, but not him? It's not fair."

Laura spread her hands. "Fair or not, being required to ride in order to bid is the hand we're being dealt. We have to decide to go all in or fold."

Emma retrieved her napkin, checking to see if it had stuck to her pork chop. "Well, I'm all in. If I can pretend to be bucked off by Willie Bite for a handful of investors, I can climb on any other bronc for a whole stadium of people."

Meira sat forward. "Do you think they will let us bring broncs from Grit and Grace to ride?"

Beth caught the thread. "That would be brilliant. We can show off how rank our broncs are and get the chance to bid all at the same time. I'm in."

"That actually is a win-win," Laura said. "If they'll agree to us bringing our own broncs to ride, I'm in, too."

All eyes looked to Sammie, waiting for her to either go all in or fold. She didn't have a choice. "I will tell them that the former Buckin' Babes will ride in an exhibition this week if we can use Grit and Grace broncs. But . . . I can't ride."

Emma placed a hand on Sammie's arm. "Is your back bad again?"

The temptation to latch on to the out Emma just gave Sammie was intense, but as she'd thought earlier, it was only a matter of time before her secret outed itself, whether she wanted it to or not. She folded her hands in her lap, her thumbs resting against her stomach.

"No," Sammie said. "It's not my back. I can't ride—at least not on a bronc—because . . . well, because I'm pregnant."

The silence around the table was deafening.

Panic erupted in Sammie's chest. Her worst fear was coming true. She was about to lose the first place she'd ever felt as if she belonged.

Then all hell broke loose.

Meira reared back. "What?!"

Emma leapt to her feet, nearly toppling her chair, and gasped, "Shut the front door!"

Beth's eyes narrowed. She pointed an accusing finger at Sammie. "I knew it! I freakin' knew it. That's why you've been eating so weird."

Laura sat back and said, "Ah. Now *that* explains why he's here."

Meira looked to Laura. "He who?"

Laura raised her brows pointedly at Sammie.

Sammie pulled in a deep breath. Time to be completely honest with everyone. "Alec Neisson. I'm pregnant with Alec Neisson's baby."

And if she wanted to be honest with herself, assuming she could form a thought over the cacophony of her friends' reactions, she'd have to also admit she was falling in love with him.

Chapter Twelve

As Beth replaced Sammie's iced sweet tea with a brimming glass of milk, Sammie fended off another helping of now-cold vegetables from Emma. Sammie wondered if she'd done the right thing by telling her friends about her pregnancy.

As well as who the father was.

Exactly what she'd made Alec promise, repeatedly, he wouldn't do.

Whatever remorse she might feel over spilling the beans was eclipsed by the overwhelming relief from having unburdened herself of such a weighty secret. Especially after Laura's gentle lecture that Grit and Grace could only succeed if they were honest with each other.

Even though her being pregnant was far more disruptive to their plans than a screwdriver to a gas tank could ever be, they were showing her complete support.

She still worried if she'd done the right thing by telling them. Right or wrong, the cat was out of the bag. She could either accept it or swear them all to secrecy.

A knife and fork in hand, Emma leaned toward Sammie and started to cut up her so-far-untouched pork chop. "You need to eat more protein, Sammie."

Sammie's heart grew two sizes at her friends' outpouring of caring. But she was a grown woman. "I got it, Emma. Really. Thanks, though." Sammie smiled and subtly moved her plate out of Emma's reach.

Meira shook her head. "She's pregnant, not injured, Emma."

"Speaking of injured," Emma said as she popped a bite of her own pork chop into her mouth. "I'm assuming you didn't really hurt your back?"

Regret settled like a rock on Sammie's shoulders as she met Emma's gaze. "No. I didn't. I'm so sorry I lied to you about why I couldn't ride Willie Bite for the investors. There's nothing wrong with me, per se. Aside from some weird food cravings and the urge to throw up at very random times, I'm fine."

Laura asked, "How far along are you?"

Beth asked at the same time, "When does the doctor think you'll be due?"

Answering Laura first, Sammie said, "Just five weeks. I haven't been sure for long."

Comprehension dawned in Laura's expressive hazel eyes. "After the Pineville Rodeo dance. You and Alec were sparking pretty hard that night."

Sammie felt her cheeks flush with embarrassment as she

nodded. She speared a piece of meat and put it in her mouth. The heat in her cheeks intensified when she admitted to Beth around the bite of pork chop, "I haven't been to a doctor yet. I haven't had the chance."

Everyone began talking at once and grabbing for their phones.

Beth shook her head and started typing into her phone. "No, no, no. We need to find you an ob-gyn here in Last Stand."

Meira said, "You've got to see a doctor ASAP, Sammie."

Laura agreed as she scrolled through her phone. "You need to start everything off on the right foot. The right vitamins, diet, rest . . ."

Sammie held up her fork in surrender. "I know, I know. I just wanted to get our first rodeo roughstock contract nailed down before I . . ." She searched for the right turn of phrase. "Shift my focus."

Beth smiled indulgently. "Your body will shift your focus for you, Sammie."

Reading off her phone, Meira said, "There's a Dr. Susan Burk who has an OB-GYN practice attached to the Gordon C. Jameson Hospital right here in Last Stand. It looks like her office is in the medical building next to, or maybe part of, the hospital. I can't tell. Let me call—"

"No," Sammie said a little too loudly. "I'll take care of it, I promise."

Her kind heart shining bright in her dark eyes, Beth said,

"I can go with you."

"Me, too," Emma said, undoubtedly motivated by her love of excitement. "Will they do an ultrasound? Will we hear the baby's heartbeat? They always show that on TV."

Her head swimming with their enthusiasm, Sammie set down her fork and laid a hand over her bursting heart. "Thank you, guys. I appreciate you all so much. But Alec has asked to go with me."

Her pronouncement was met with wide smiles and knowing looks exchanged around the table.

Beth sighed. "That's so romantic."

Emma made a rude noise. "Romantic, my butt. He knocked her up. The least he can do is go with her to the doctor. And pay for everything. Which shouldn't be a problem, considering he's Thomas Wright's grandson."

A surge of something closely resembling protectiveness raised Sammie's heart rate. "Last I looked, it takes two to tango. I bear just as much responsibility for what happened between Alec and me." She picked up her fork again and aggressively speared a piece of pork. "I'd wanted that night with Alec. And I want this baby. He deserved the right to know I was pregnant, just like he deserves the right to be a part of our baby's life. But I don't need his help. Nor do I need, or want, his money. I intend to have and raise this baby on my own."

Emma reached for Sammie, laying a firm hand on Sammie's forearm to fully capture her attention. "You will never be on your own, Sammie. You have us."

Tears sprung to Sammie's eyes and her vision blurred.

The other women around the table concurred with Emma.

"That's right," Meira said.

Beth stood and hurried around the table. Wrapping her arms around Sammie's shoulders, she said, "We'll always be here for you, Sammie."

At the same time, Laura said, "You can't get rid of us."

Sammie's throat closed up tight. She could only nod her thanks, patting Beth's arm in appreciation. How had she come to deserve such friendship?

Emma grinned broadly and released Sammie's arm with an encouraging pat. "Now that's settled, eat your pork chop."

Beth released her. "Yes, eat. I can get you something else if none of this appeals to you. You liked the meatloaf. I can make you another meatloaf sandwich."

Sammie waved her off. "No, really. This is good." She smiled and proved it by placing the bite already on her fork in her mouth and chewed. Thinking again of the promise she'd extracted from Alec, she swallowed and said, "Y'all can do something for me right now."

"What?" Emma asked.

Beth sat forward. "Anything."

Laura and Meira nodded.

Sammie set her fork down again. "Can we keep my . . .

situation just between us? Well, and Alec, of course."

"And the doctor you're going to see," Laura interjected.

Sammie indicated her agreement. "And the doctor. Of course."

"Why?" Meira asked.

"First off, I don't want to land our first contract simply because I'm pregnant with Thomas Wright's great-grandchild."

Meira sat back. "Valid."

"Second, Alec needs to tell his family before this—" Sammie glanced down. "Goes wide."

Laura said, "Good enough reason. Mum's the word."

The other women, almost simultaneously, pressed their lips together and pretended to turn a key.

Sammie smiled her thanks and wondered how she'd gotten so lucky to have such wonderful friends.

ALEC PROPPED HIS coffee cup on the paddock rail and squinted against the rising sun to watch the giant, tan-and-white-speckled longhorn bull sniff the air, which was already growing warm despite the early hour. The big guy, named Bango, according to Justin, was probably trying to locate a lady love. Normally, Alec would have sympathized. But this morning he knew exactly where his lady love was. She was in the big house on the crest of the gentle rise behind him, hopefully getting the rest she needed.

Alec marveled at the sensation just the thought of Sammie created inside of him. Never in his life had he felt so . . . full.

He'd actually managed a good night's sleep, finally feeling as though he'd made some headway with Sammie. Even though she didn't trust him enough to share more of her history with him, a bubble of hope had lodged in his chest after their trip to the rodeo grounds and the breakfast they'd shared together yesterday. There was no doubt his feelings for her were growing.

He considered his options as he took a sip of the potent coffee Carlos had made before heading out to ride the fence. Alec could back off, bide his time. Wait for Sammie to realize he wasn't going anywhere. That she could, indeed, trust him to stick around for her and their baby. Let her decide when to tell him more about herself. When *another time* would be.

Backing off would not be easy, though. Especially when he could think of nothing besides taking her in his arms and never letting go. And he couldn't wait much longer to tell his family about her pregnancy. As she'd illustrated by telling him what she'd learned on the internet about his mother, it was tough in this day and age to keep much of anything a secret. The news would make its way to his family sooner or later. He'd prefer they hear about the pregnancy from him.

Just as he'd prefer the women of Grit and Grace didn't

have to trade an exhibition of bronc riding for a chance to have their roughstock bid considered. He wondered if Sammie's partners had agreed to the condition. He supposed he'd find out soon enough.

Bango blew out a noisy, wet breath and dropped his head to investigate the hay strewn on the dusty ground of the paddock, his blunted horns making it easier for the bull to snuffle around the fence posts. Maybe it was time to see what Bango thought of a bucking chute. Grit and Grace needed rank bulls to make it in today's rodeo roughstock contractor world. Alec downed the remainder of his coffee and turned from the paddock.

Emma slammed into him full force, knocking him back a step. The petite platinum blonde wrapped her arms around him, trapping his arms at his side as she hugged him tighter than a burrowed-in tick.

Stunned, all he could say was, "Wha—?"

She squealed, then said, "I'm so excited!" She released him and stepped back, winked, then took off toward the bronc barn, her white-blonde ponytail bouncing wildly.

Seriously confused, Alec just stood there.

The other women were coming down from the main house in a group, chattering away, with Beth leading the way. They were dressed for ranch work, without a sequin or rhinestone among them, but they still dazzled.

Sammie most of all, the gleam of her honey-blonde hair eye-catching even in a ponytail. The wash-worn, baby-blue

T-shirt, a shade lighter and ending an inch higher than her jeans, hugged her breasts. He stared. He couldn't help himself.

Beth called to him, "Kittens?"

Alec gestured with his empty coffee cup toward the equipment barn where Justin had set the new family up in a flannel shirt-lined box. Had Emma nearly tackled him because of a batch of kittens?

"Thanks, Pops." Beth saluted him and headed at a jog in the direction of the equipment barn.

Pops? He wasn't that much older than Beth.

Laura and Meira, with Sammie a step behind, continued toward him.

Laura extended her hand for him to shake. "Congratulations, Alec."

He set his coffee cup atop the nearest fence post to accept her handshake.

Meira clapped him on the shoulder. "Be good to her." There was a distinct warning in the beautiful woman's tone.

Understanding dawned on Alec, and his heart started to pound. He met Sammie's warm blue eyes. "You told them?"

She gave him a quick dip of her chin, the prettiest blush staining her high cheekbones and a slight smile on her full mouth. "Last night after I told them about Gene Bauer insisting on us giving an exhibition at this year's rodeo in exchange for a chance to bid for next year. Had to explain why I won't be climbing on a bronc for a good while."

Laura released Alec's hand. "At least eight months."

Sammie smiled at her friend. "Give or take."

Alec looked to Laura and Meira. "You're riding in this year's rodeo?"

Laura spread her hands. "Girls gotta do what girls gotta do."

Meira wagged a finger at Laura. "Women. What women gotta do." Meira shifted her finger and pointed at Sammie as Meira started walking toward the entrance to the bull barn attached to the paddock Bango was in. "Don't forget to make that doctor's appointment."

Laura nodded in agreement. "You two coordinate." She pointed at Sammie, then Alec. "I'll be helping Emma if you need me. Right after I play with the kittens, that is." She grinned and walked toward the equipment barn.

Alec watched Sammie as her gaze followed Laura's departure. Sammie's face glowed with what looked to be contentment. That glow drew him to her as effectively as a lassoed calf.

He knew he should resist the impulse.

He didn't want to.

He closed the gap between them with two long strides and settled a hand on her jeans-clad hip, his index finger and thumb landing on hot bare skin. He said quietly, "A good thing?"

She looked up at him and her smile softened. "Telling them?"

He nodded and his hand slid upward to fully grasp her bare waist, his gaze stuck on her tempting mouth. She hadn't applied any of her trademark lip gloss this morning, making her naturally pink, oh-so-kissable mouth irresistible.

"Yes. A very good thing." Obviously aware of his focus on her mouth, she pressed her lips together, then ruined the apparent discouragement by moistening her lips with her tongue.

A smile tugging at his own mouth, he shifted his attention and reached up to finger a blonde curl she'd missed when pulling her hair into a low ponytail. The strand was pure silk and reminded him of the ecstasy of having his hands buried in her hair as they made love. He was forced to swallow hard before he could say, "I'm glad."

"So am I," she breathed out, her voice husky.

He reluctantly released the curl. It sprang back up to frame her heart-shaped face. "Can I tell my family now?"

Her gaze jumped from where she'd been watching his mouth to his eyes.

Alec registered her awareness south of his belt buckle and his stomach contracted.

She blinked slowly, then said, "Yes. You probably should."

"Good. Great." He licked his suddenly tingly lips.

Her eyes flared with heat in the blue depths.

Bango bellowed, low and forlornly, reminding Alec they were standing out in the open next to a bull corral. He released her hip and stepped back. "The *you two should coordinate* remark...?" He retrieved the coffee cup from atop the fence post and gestured in the direction Laura had gone.

A rueful smile curved her lips. "A couple—well, all—of them offered to go with me to see an ob-gyn in Last Stand we found online last night, but I told them you wanted to go with me."

His chest swelled with pleasure. "I do."

"So... we should coordinate." Her tone was tentative, despite his obvious enthusiasm to be involved in this journey she was on.

"I'm free." Not just to go with her to a doctor's appointment, but to be with her. For the rest of his life. He decided to keep the sentiment to himself.

"When?"

"Anytime you need me. Whenever you can get an appointment, I'll be free."

The corner of her very kissable mouth twitched upward. "Convenient."

He automatically shifted back toward her, his brain filled with the memory of her satiny skin, the little moans of pleasure that had sent his ego soaring. "That's me. Mr. Convenient."

Her burgeoning smile vanished, and a scoff sounded deep in her elegant, kissable throat. "Not really."

Stung, Alec eased back, the spell broken. "How so?"

She arched an eyebrow as if he'd had his head stepped on one time too many. "Alec Neisson, Thomas Wright's grandson? Of the Wright Ranch, a massive competitor of what we're trying to build here?"

Alec had no argument. She was stating the obvious. "I can't help who my family is or what they do for a living. Any more than I can change the fact that I made you pregnant."

She huffed out an irritated-sounding breath. "*We* made me pregnant. Both of us. I was a willing participant."

Alec pulled off his cowboy hat and started to shove a hand through his hair, but realized he still held his empty coffee cup. He ended up gesturing with both his hat and cup. "Yeah, but—"

"There are no '*yeah, buts*,' Alec. We didn't plan for me to get pregnant, but I am. It happened. Now we deal with the reality." She reached up a hand and patted him on the chest, missing his heart with her hand, but not her words. "I'll let you know when I have an appointment."

He planted his hat back on his head. "Please do." He tried to trap her hand against his chest with his own, but she snatched hers away and stepped back.

"I will. I need to go help Emma with the broncs." She turned and started walking to the bronc barn.

He almost called out *be careful*, but luckily, came to his senses.

She'd only taken a few steps away when the cell phone she had tucked in her back pocket rang. She stopped to answer the call.

"Yes, this is she. Oh, hello, Mr. Bauer." Sammie turned to face Alec, her expression expectant.

He drifted toward her.

"Okay, Gene," she half-laughed, having obviously been told to be less formal with good-ol'-boy Gene. "What can I do for you?"

Alec stopped in front of her, watching her listen to what Gene was saying. Her dark-blonde brows came together. Alec couldn't quite make out what Gene's part of the conversation, but clearly Sammie wasn't liking what she was hearing. His need to protect her reared up and he started to reach for the phone.

She held up a finger that was both a warning and a request for patience. "Tomorrow?" She heaved a sigh. "Yes, we can do that. And four of us can ride in the exhibition. If—" Her gaze met his, her blue eyes glinting with determination. "We can ride Grit and Grace broncs."

Ah. Attagirl.

She listened for a moment longer, then said, "Okay. Thank you. Yes. See you tomorrow."

Alec waited for her to hit the red button on her phone to end the call, then raised his eyebrows at her. "Will he let you ride Grit and Grace broncs?"

She smiled. "He will."

Alec relaxed a little. "That's good."

"But . . ." She returned her cell phone to the back pocket

of her jeans.

"But?"

Sammie tucked the lock of hair he'd touched earlier behind her ear. "He wants us to ride in the parade the day before the rodeo."

"The day . . . You mean, tomorrow?"

"That would be tomorrow."

Alec thought for a minute. "Asher has some nice saddle horses and tack. Definitely parade worthy. I'll check and make sure there are four mounts that are well shod."

"Five."

"Pardon?"

"We need five saddle horses. I'm riding in the parade, too."

Alec shook his head, slowly at first, then building up speed. "Not until you've been given the go-ahead by a doc."

Sammie made a face. "I'm perfectly fine. I can ride. I might have to hook a barf bag on my saddle horn, but other than that . . ."

Alec's jaw tightened. "No, Sammie. Not until you've been seen by an ob-gyn."

Sammie made a very impressive, very rude noise and wheeled away from him, pulling her phone back out and typing on it as she paced away.

Alec crossed his arms over his chest and waited. He knew from his sister's experience that healthy pregnant women could ride, but only after receiving the 'all clear' from their obstetrician. This was one thing Alec would not budge on.

He watched Sammie make a call, continuing to pace back and forth about twenty feet away from him. When she ended the call, she stomped back to him.

"This afternoon at 4:45. You free?"

He spread his arms wide and winked. "Mr. Convenient, remember?"

Chapter Thirteen

HIS PHONE IN his hand, Alec stood in the aisle of the extensively remodeled and upgraded stable where the saddle horses Asher Halliday had purchased were kept for use at the A Bar H. Built of the same multi-colored Hill Country sandstone as the main house and bunkhouse, the stable had been expanded and updated with what looked to be reclaimed, dark-stained timber and scrolled wrought iron that gave the long building a distinct Southwest flair. The high dormer windows that made the interior well lit reminded Alec of the saddle horse stable back home at the Wright Ranch.

Just like everything on this ranch being only the best money could buy, Halliday had chosen only the best quarter horses to grace his stable. Carlos had taken an ATV earlier this morning to check the fences, so all six saddle horses were still in their stalls, waiting to be ridden or put out to pasture for the day.

Justin ran a tight ship, so Alec wasn't worried about the horses being well shod, but considering who would be riding the horses on pavement in the middle of a noisy Fourth of July rodeo parade, he needed to make sure.

First, though, Alec needed to call his family with the news there was another addition to the Neisson clan on the way. He checked the time on his phone, taking the two-hour difference between Texas and Oregon into account. Everyone at home should be up.

But who to call?

The anxiety born of an uncertainty that had been simmering deep in Alec's gut ever since Sammie had given him the green light to tell his family flared. He opened his contacts and scrolled through his family members' names and numbers.

Alec's jangling nerves made him automatically skip Thomas Wright. His finger hovered over Douglas Neisson. Dad would be the obvious first choice, but only with good news. Which Sammie's pregnancy was, but not necessarily under the best circumstances. While the entire family had been devastated by Mom's injury and death, Dad had taken the loss the hardest. An integral part of him had been severed. He'd never been the same, and the entire family made an effort to shield him from upset now.

Alec's oldest brother, Ian, had stepped up and filled the hole their dad had unintentionally left, but his black and white way of looking at things made telling him first less appealing. Same with Alec's second oldest brother, Liam, though marriage had softened him. Their lone sister, Caitlin, would be happy for him and Sammie, but she'd want to be involved in everything and she already had her hands full with her own growing family.

Which left Drew, the sibling closest to Alec in more than just age. As Peyton Halliday's fiancé, Drew would also be the best family member to spread the news. Peyton and Sammie had been close when they were on the *Buckin' Babes* reality TV show, and Peyton was part of the Grit and Grace operation, though in absentia.

Alec scrolled to Drew's name and number, but he hesitated. Drew was also a doctor. Of sports medicine, but he'd nevertheless want all the medical-type details. Details Alec didn't have yet.

He clicked off his phone's screen and tucked it into his jeans' back pocket. He would call his family after Sammie's appointment with the obstetrician later this afternoon.

Until then, he would check out the horses and tack the women would use in the parade tomorrow, picking out the mellowest mount in the bunch for Sammie to ride if the doctor gave the okay.

DRESSED AGAIN AFTER her exam and waiting for the doctor's return with the test results, Sammie let Alec into the small room she'd been seen in at the ob-gyn's. Thankfully, neither the nurse nor the doctor commented on Sammie and Alec's mutual yet silent agreement that he should remain in the hall during her exam.

His cowboy hat in his hands, Alec took a seat in the corner of the room on a blue plastic chair, looking huge and out of place, while Sammie perched on the edge of the exam table. The protective paper crinkled and tore beneath her. She had never felt more awkward in her life.

Alec's blue eyes were dark with concern. "How are you?"

Not *how did the exam go*, or *what did the doctor say*. His thoughts were of her. He cared about how she was doing.

Sammie's throat grew tight. She had to clear it to speak. "I'm okay. It was okay. Dr. Burk seems nice. I like her."

"Do you think she's any good? That she knows what she's doing?"

Sammie shrugged. "I guess. I don't know. How do you know?"

Clearly picking up on her rising anxiety, Alec said, "It's okay, Sammie. I'm sure she's good."

"If I'd had more time, I could have done some research, I guess, but you insisted that I be checked out before I—"

Alec quickly stood, placed his hat on the chair, and moved to stand in front of her. She automatically opened her jeans-clad legs to him. He gathered her hands in his. "It's okay, Sammie. I'm just a little nervous too."

Before she could think of what to say, a quick knock sounded on the exam room door a second before it opened and Dr. Burk entered. Perhaps in her early forties, the doctor was attractive, with sandy-blonde hair cut in an asymmetrical bob. She held an electronic tablet in one hand and a handled plastic bag in the other.

Her gaze landed on Sammie and Alec's joined hands, and her smile widened as she closed the door behind her. "Well, good news. You are indeed pregnant. With a due date of February seventh."

Alec squeezed Sammie's hands, then released her and moved from between her legs to her side, hitching a hip onto the exam table.

Dr. Burk consulted her tablet. "Your physical exam and blood work look good, with your hCG—" She glanced up at them. "The pregnancy hormone—levels strong for this stage. Which explains why you're experiencing morning sickness already. But I don't think the level is high enough to suggest multiples."

Multiples? Panic surging through her, Sammie glanced at Alec. He looked a little white around the mouth. She returned her attention to the doctor. "Multiples as in . . .?"

Dr. Burk smiled indulgently. "Twins. Or more. But your hCG would typically be double what I'm seeing here, so I'm thinking you'll only need to add one pony to your stable."

Sammie relaxed considerably. Twins! She hadn't even considered the possibility. They, at least, had dodged that bullet. The doctor went on to discuss when she'd like to see Sammie again for an ultrasound and other routine care.

Dr. Burk said, "Okay, that's my spiel. Do either of you

have any questions for me?" She looked expectantly between them.

Realizing she hadn't asked the question that had brought her to the doctor in a rush, she said, "Can I ride a saddle horse?"

At the exact same time, Alec asked, "Is it okay if she has sex?"

Shocked, Sammie gaped at Alec.

Appearing not shocked in the slightest, Dr. Burk said, "Funny enough, those are the two questions I'm asked most in these parts." She pointed at Sammie. "In answer to your question, yes. If you trust your mount and you don't try anything too crazy."

She aimed her finger at Alec. "As for your question . . ." She grinned. "Same answer."

Alec snorted a laugh.

Her cheeks growing hot, Sammie sent him what she hoped to be a quelling glare. How could he be thinking about that now, of all times? And now she was thinking about it, too, darn him.

Dr. Burk held out the plastic bag to Sammie. "Here is your prenatal welcome package, with all sorts of info in the form of a booklet and pamphlets, a sample of prenatal vitamins that I want you to start on right away, and coupons for goodies you never knew you needed."

Her cheeks flaming after automatically picturing the doctor's answer to sex with Alec, Sammie took the handled plastic bag from Dr. Burk. "Thank you, Doctor."

Dr. Burk inclined her head. "You're welcome. I look forward to traveling this adventurous trail with you two. Stop at the reception desk on your way out and schedule your next visits and the ultrasound."

The doctor bid them goodbye and left the room.

Sammie slipped off the exam table and turned to Alec. "I told you I would be okay to ride."

Alec looked down at her, his gaze full of banked heat and his smile just a little wicked. "Indeed."

ALEC DROVE HIS truck through town away from the medical center, his attention less on the road and more on the woman seated in the passenger seat next to him. She had been acting almost shy since they left Dr. Burk's office.

Undoubtedly because he'd opened his yap and asked the question he'd had no right asking. He wasn't her husband. He wasn't even her boyfriend. At the moment, all he was to her was a competitor and the father of the baby growing within her.

He wanted to be so much more. While he'd know he hadn't been ready to let her go since the morning after their night together when he'd woken up alone, the extent of his desire to be more hadn't quite hit him until he'd been standing in the hall during her obstetrics exam.

He wanted a relationship with Sammie "Don't call me Samantha" Abel.

Judging by the way she'd avoided his gaze since they left the doctor's office, he might have set himself back in the winning-Sammie-over quest with his sex question.

He'd embarrassed her. But he had to admit he'd been a little caught up in the fantasy of being a real couple with Sammie at the doctor appointment.

And inquiring minds wanted to know.

Alec glanced at Sammie. She stared out the windshield, the plastic bag containing a booklet, pamphlets, prenatal samples, and coupons gripped tightly in both hands. He could take the easy route and pretend he'd never said a word about them having intimate relations again.

Or he could see if she was game.

He sure as hell was.

Alec's heart rate picked up and his temperature started to rise, among other things, at the thought.

Because he cared for her, more so every day. Whether they explored more deeply whatever it was between them would be Sammie's choice.

But there was nothing wrong with trying to nudge her in his direction.

"Hungry?" he asked her.

She glanced at him, her eyebrows up, then quickly looked away. "I could eat." She readjusted her hold on the plastic bag. "Won't guarantee whatever I eat will stay down, though."

"How about if I stop and grab something to go?"

She smiled at him. "That would be great."

Alec's heart lifted. He made a turn and drove down Main Street, nabbing an angled parking spot directly in front of the statue of Asa Fuhrmann, a Last Stand hero who'd given his life protecting the town from Mexican troops during the Texas Revolution. At least according to the plaque affixed to the statue. Alec left the truck running.

"I'll leave the AC on, so you don't cook. Be right back," he told Sammie, then jumped from the truck and jogged across the street to Hutchinson's BBQ Market. Though they only provided food service during lunch hours, Alec was able to buy two premade roast beef sandwiches with nothing fancy on them, to avoid triggering her nausea, and two bottles of water.

When Alec returned to the truck, he found Sammie reading one of the booklets the doctor had given her.

"Light reading?" he asked as he climbed in, setting the bag with the sandwiches between them. He put the truck in gear and backed out of the parking spot.

"More like a horror story." She flipped the booklet closed and shoved it back into the plastic bag.

Alec cringed with sympathy and a hearty dose of contrition. But what was done was done. However, there was one thing he'd like to do again.

Sammie's attention went to the bag between them.

"What'cha get?"

"Roast beef sandwiches and water." He glanced at her as he drove out of town. "Hope that's okay?"

She carefully opened the folded top of the paper bag as if it might contain rattlesnakes. Leaning toward the bag, she took a tentative sniff and waited.

She looked at him and grinned. "Good choice."

His chest loosened. "Thank goodness. I'd hate to make you puke."

"I'm sure it will happen eventually." She pulled out a bottled water and took a sip. "Are you thinking we wait and eat at the ranch, or is it okay to eat in your brand-spankin'-new truck?"

"Neither. I know of a perfect spot for a picnic. If you're game, that is."

He could feel her watching him as he drove. He shifted his attention to her.

She smiled. Everything about her seemed softened toward him. "Yeah, I'm game."

Alec returned her smile, falling headlong into the warmth in her eyes. No one would ever accuse him of not being up for taking a risk. Especially if it involved Sammie.

AS ALEC DROVE his truck down a dirt track just inside the fence marking the town-side boundary of the A Bar H Ranch toward what Sammie assumed to be his picnic spot, the heavy-duty shocks handling the bumps and ruts with ease, she could only think of one thing . . .

Alec had wanted to know if it was safe for her to have sex. Assumingly with him. Of course, with him. He was a true-blue, dyed-in-the-wool cowboy, raised in The Cowboy Way.

Men like Alec didn't share.

A zing of electricity traveled through her with enough force to curl her hair as well as her toes. There was no doubt the idea of being claimed by Alec turned her on.

The exact same idea had sent her running five weeks ago.

There was no running from the connection she had with him now, though. She was pregnant with his child. He would always be in her life from here on out. Was it so wrong for her to hope for more from him than just being the father of her child?

She'd felt shellshocked by his question in the doctor's office. Now . . .? Now she was tempted.

So very tempted.

Tempted by the breadth of his shoulders and the strength of his convictions. By the sparkle of humor in his blue eyes. By the passion in even the quickest of his kisses or his hand on the bare skin of her waist. Everything about Alec Neisson tempted her to set aside her fears and nod for the gate to the rest of their lives to be flung open.

She could always resist the temptation. Climb out of the

saddle. Refuse the ride by continuing to push him away.

Or she could give in, acknowledging her own wants, and embracing what he was willing to give her for however long he'd give it. Grab the chance to stick with it until the buzzer sounded.

Sammie worried her lip as Alec pulled his truck beneath a huge, ancient live oak growing alone on a slight rise. The tall grass, just starting to yellow under the summer sun, swayed gently in the slight, refreshing breeze.

He shut off the truck and turned to her, a question swimming in his blue eyes.

Her heart answered.

She smiled at him. "This is the perfect spot."

He grinned. "I think so, too."

She grabbed her water and the bag of food before climbing from his truck. Alec pulled a red-and-black-checked wool blanket from behind the seat and joined her on a flat spot at the base of the sprawling oak tree's trunk. After spreading the blanket, Alec took the food bag from her and encouraged her to take a seat. He eased down next to her, and they both took a moment to soak in the view.

The knoll that the A Bar H's main house, with its pool, bunkhouse, stable, and barns, was built on was slightly lower than where they sat, and Sammie was struck anew by how wonderful her new home was.

"Wow," Sammie breathed out.

"Not gonna lie, that is one hell of a ranch." Alec nodded,

his appreciation for his brother's soon-to-be brother-in-law's creation clear.

After silently enjoying the view for a moment, Alec pulled a butcher paper-wrapped sandwich from the bag and handed it to Sammie. She opened her sandwich and took a few bites, thinking.

Risking sharing at least one of her fears with Alec, she said, "I sure hope Asher Halliday doesn't decide to kick us off anytime soon."

Alec pulled out his own sandwich, unwrapped it, and took a bite. "He won't," he said around the mouthful. He chewed and swallowed before continuing. "He wouldn't have offered it for lease to you guys if he thought he might want to live here all of a sudden."

Said with the confidence of a man who called an equally amazing ranch home. In Oregon.

Though she'd already decided to give in to the temptation that was Alec, she found herself asking, "Where do you intend to live, Alec?"

His mouth full of another big bite of sandwich and his attention on the amazing view below them, Alec didn't hesitate. "Wherever you are, Sammie."

The earth shifted beneath Sammie.

No one had ever, in her entire life, given her such a gift of hope.

Grasping for the metaphorical saddle horn to keep her emotional seat, Sammie took a long drink from her water bottle, wrapped up the remainder of her sandwich in its wrapper, and shifted to face Alec. "Really?"

He stopped just as he was about to take another bite and looked at her. Something in her expression made his eyebrows hitch upward. He quickly shoved his sandwich back in the bag and moved it from between them, off to the side of the large blanket.

He cupped her face in his hands and looked into her soul. "Yes, Sammie. I will never lie to you. I intend to be in our baby's life. And in yours, if you'll let me. I wanted to be in your life even before you told me you're pregnant."

Sammie's heart exploded with something she'd never dared hope to experience. "Oh, Alec." She gripped his shoulders, pulling him nearer.

He kissed her in a way he hadn't before. No flirty fun, studied skill, superficial, stolen pleasure. She felt his heart in his kiss. She felt his hope for a future together.

An explosion of passion born of a maturity possible only through the creation of another life.

His kiss, deep and passionate, spoke of a bond they shared. One she didn't want to break.

Alec eased her back onto the blanket without breaking the kiss. Impossibly, he deepened it, shifting his weight toward her. Sammie moved one hand from his shoulder to his hip, then to his perfectly formed cowboy butt, yanking him onto her.

He didn't resist, shifting his weight, his hardness, onto

her.

Sammie moaned.

Alec broke off the kiss in response, moving back enough to meet her gaze. "Are you sure?"

"Yes. I'm sure." A ridiculous thought occurred to her, and she laughed. "It's not like I can get any more pregnant, Alec."

Something akin to panic flared in his eyes, and he started to pull back.

Sammie wasn't having it. This was no time for chivalry or squeamishness or whatever was going through that cowboy brain of his. She tightened her grip on his butt and held him close. "Alec. I thought you were game. The doctor said I can. I trust you. And I promise not to try anything too crazy."

His body and expression relaxed. His slow smile made her heart nearly explode. "As long as you're sure."

She hooked a leg over his jean-clad calf and pulled him closer still, fitting their parts together. Perfectly. "I am."

So Alec proceeded to make slow yet intense love to Sammie under the sheltering branches of an old oak tree, the early July Texas sun filtering through the tree's thick canopy of leaves as it began its descent.

And Sammie decided she had chosen wisely.

Chapter Fourteen

THE NEXT MORNING, the field behind Last Stand's high school served as the Fourth of July Rodeo kick-off parade's hectic staging area. Alec rechecked the front cinch on the saddle he'd placed on the back of the beautiful cream buckskin quarter horse he had insisted Sammie ride. The temperature was already inching up as the sun climbed in the cloudless sky.

Yesterday, after he'd had a taste of heaven under an ancient oak tree with Sammie and then seen her safely to the main house, he'd gone straight to the stable. He'd wanted to take one more look at the saddle horses and make his final choice of which one he thought Sammie should ride in the parade.

The doctor had said Sammie could ride a trusted mount. He needed to build that trust. For both the horse and himself.

All the horses Asher had purchased for the ranch were of excellent quality and had been expertly trained. Justin had provided exceptional care for the animals before and after the women had leased the ranch.

Alec wanted Sammie mounted on a horse with a calm and steady temperament, one that wouldn't be spooked by the cacophony that was a popular pre-rodeo parade the week of the Fourth of July. There would be drums, horns, and cymbals from the high school bands, random fireworks from those who couldn't wait until the actual Fourth, and general whooping and hollering from pretty much everyone. Overall, not a great environment for what was essentially a prey animal.

Cedar, a heavy chested eight-year-old buckskin gelding, fit the bill exactly. No amount of bucket-clanging or high-pitched whistles had ruffled the big guy.

Smoothing a hand down Cedar's shiny, pitch-black mane, Alec turned to see if the former Buckin' Babes, who he now thought of as the women of Grit and Grace, were ready to climb aboard their respective mounts, currently tended to by Justin and Carlos. The women had been signing autographs and posing for photos with a surprising number of fans here in Last Stand. A television camera crew from an Austin TV station was busy taping them.

The ladies had done themselves up to an impressive extent. Standing all together, they would sparkle even in the dead of night, so in the bright morning sun, the rhinestones and sequins adorning their jeans, fringed western shirts, and hatbands would rival a disco ball. He was pretty sure they even had some sort of multi-colored tinsel woven into their long, loosely curled hair, in every color featured in teenage males' dreams, hanging free beneath their hats that were white, tan, brown, and black.

As lovely as the ladies were as a group, Alec had eyes only for one. Tall and lissome, Sammie was stunning in black jeans with heavily bedazzled pockets beneath matching chaps. Combined with a black, fringed-sleeved western shirt and a black hat, her long blonde hair was beautiful. While he hadn't known beforehand what she'd be wearing, he realized she would be breathtaking aboard Cedar, with his creamy tan coat, black mane, tail, and lower legs. Alec's chest swelled with a ridiculous amount of pride. He couldn't help but think of her as his. And not just because she was the mother of his child. He claimed every inch of her. He wanted to spend his life worshiping Sammie Abel.

Alec couldn't wait to tell it to the world. Or, at least to start, his brother Drew. Alec had tried calling him last night but had reached voicemail. He'd left a message asking Drew to call him and had yet to hear back. He pulled his cell phone from his pocket to check if he'd missed a call or if there was a text message from his brother.

Nothing.

Drew was undoubtedly tending to banged-up cowboys and cowgirls in his sports medicine mobile clinic at a rodeo somewhere similar to Last Stand. Alec would try again after the parade.

Then he would broach the subject of the future with

Sammie. Maybe she'd be willing to return to Oregon with him to help run his grandfather's bucking bull program. He wouldn't know until he asked.

A parade organizer, identifiable by her clipboard and frazzled demeanor, shooed the women to their mounts. They were to follow, at a sensible distance, a group of children riding Fourth of July-decorated bikes, trikes, and wagons. Behind the women from Grit and Grace would be a crew of pooper scoopers dressed as frontiersmen, or maybe they were supposed to be the brave men who participated in the last stand for which this town was named.

Alec was again thankful he'd tested Cedar for any sensitivity to loud noises because several of the children's bikes and trikes had bells attached and were already being enthusiastically put to use. Luckily, the other horses from the A Bar H seemed to be taking the chaos in stride as well. So far.

Sammie strode toward Alec and Cedar, and Alec's mind went blank. Then she smiled at him, a look filled with memory and promise, and he went up in flames. His hands flexed. Alec had to grab on to his control to keep from scooping her into his arms and carrying her somewhere quiet for a repeat performance of last evening.

When she reached him, he asked, "You ready for this?"

"I am. Please don't worry. This isn't my first rodeo parade."

Fully intending to worry, he smiled. "Just keep your seat. That's all I ask."

She placed a too-quick kiss on his lips. "I will. Then you can keep it all you want."

Certain steam was coming out of his ears, he stepped back and held Cedar's rein while she fit her boot into the stirrup and swung herself up into the saddle with practiced ease. She gathered the reins into her left hand.

Alec checked the length of the stirrup. "Along with the bag of candy for you to throw to the kids . . ." He patted the small canvas bag hooked over the saddle horn. "Just in case, I tucked a plastic emergency barf bag under the pommel."

Sammie's smile softened and her eyes grew watery as she looked down at him. "You know, I think that's the sweetest thing anyone has ever done for me."

Alec laughed. "Talk about a low bar. This is going to be stupid easy."

"This?"

"Wooing you down from your high tower."

She scoffed and rolled her eyes. "Oh please. Come here, you," Sammie said and leaned down and grabbed his collar, pulling him close to kiss him.

This time there was nothing quick about it. She kissed him with the same soul-warming passion as she had under the oak tree. He did his damnedest to return the favor with a hand hooked around her neck, trying to convey all the emotions crowding his chest.

Behind him Emma called, "Save it for later, you two. Time to smile and wave, Sammie."

Sammie smiled against his lips, and he reluctantly released her. She straightened away from him and settled into the saddle. Cedar was so well trained, Sammie only needed to slightly lift the reins to send him in motion. She guided the gorgeous gelding to where her friends and their mounts had lined up, ready to be sent onto the parade route.

Only then did Alec notice the camera crew now filming him.

Uh-oh. Drew had better return Alec's call soon, on the off chance his grandfather was watching for any news of what was going on in Last Stand, Texas.

SAMMIE'S SMILE WAS genuine as she rode Cedar slowly down Last Stand's Main Street. In between throwing wrapped candies to the kids, she gave her best parade wave to the cheering crowds gathered along the curbs, braving the hot early-July sun for a day of fun in a town that had managed to retain much of its Old West charm through the years.

Elbow elbow, wrist wrist.

She glanced at her friends riding next to her on Asher Halliday's top-shelf quarter horses. If you have the money, then you buy the best, she guessed. They all looked like they belonged on such quality mounts, though, holding themselves with the ease that comes from practice and maturity.

Not to mention a hearty dose of reality TV experience.

The Last Stand Rodeo queen and her court had nothing on the former Buckin' Babes.

While they all had every right to be sullen, having been blackmailed into participating in the parade and doing an exhibition during the rodeo in exchange for the chance to bid for a contract to supply rough stock for next year's rodeo, their smiles appeared genuine.

Sammie's sure was. Her lips still tingled from Alec's kisses.

Hell, other parts of her were tingling from their soul-touching tryst under the old oak tree the evening before. She could easily blame the pregnancy hormones for the depth of emotion she'd felt, that she continued to feel, but she wasn't sure doing so would be fair to Alec. For what seemed to be the millionth time, she thought the guy was amazing. He made her feel amazing.

The acknowledgement should freak her out, make her want to push him away, shut him out, ghost him like she had the first time.

But things were different now. She reached into the hole between the saddle horn and seat until her fingers encountered the plastic, just-in-case barf bag Alec had tucked in the space. Her heart warmed.

She was different now. She was pregnant with Alec Neisson's baby, and she didn't regret it.

Today was a beautiful day. She was in a beautiful place with amazing people. She was riding a beautiful horse picked especially for her by a man who seemed to care about her.

And she cared about him. *Really* cared about him.

So Sammie decided to enjoy the day, revel in all the positive attention being given to her and worry about the future later.

Thanks to Cedar's seemingly easy acceptance of the raucous atmosphere surrounding them, Sammie was completely relaxed in the saddle and barely gripped the reins, allowing them to hang slack as she continued to toss wrapped candies to the children, and obvious children-at-heart, in the crowd.

Out of the corning of her eye, Sammie saw something sail over the curbside crowd, trailing a thin line of white smoke, landing in the street directly in front of the horses. Cedar's head lifted and his ears pricked forward.

Sammie identified the short strand of lady finger firecrackers, connected by a single fuse, a bare second before they erupted in a series of earsplitting and sparking mini explosions. She instinctively grabbed hold of the saddle horn.

Emma and Beth's horses screamed and reared, while Laura's mount wheeled with the intent of fleeing in the opposite direction. The horse Meira was riding skittered sideways, slamming into Cedar's haunch and just missing Sammie's leg. Cedar didn't budge an inch, having dropped his head low and widened his stance the way any good cutting horse does when waiting to see which way a steer will try to bolt. As the firecrackers continued to pop and jump, Cedar eased backward, creating space between them and the noisy, yet harmless, explosions.

Recognizing that her mount wasn't going to panic, Sammie glanced around to check on her friends. Thanks to their extensive experience riding occasionally rank bucking broncs, all the women had successfully kept their seats and were battling to get their horses under control. Luckily, the children ahead of them and the spectators nearest them, as well as the trooper pooper scoopers, had scattered the moment the fireworks erupted, leaving room for the women to settle their mounts.

A quick-thinking mom ran into the street and dumped a large soda on the now-spent but still smoking remains of the firecrackers. Alec appeared out of nowhere, dodging a toppled lawn chair to get to the middle of the street and use his boots to stomp the fireworks into complete submission.

With Last Stand being a town full of cowboys and cowgirls, there was plenty of help from the crowd settling the horses while others asked if anyone had seen who'd thrown the fireworks in the first place.

The threat subdued, Alec came immediately to Sammie and Cedar, unnecessarily gripping the horse's bridle. "Are you okay?" he asked calmly enough, given Sammie could see how hard he was breathing.

"I'm fine. Where did you come from?"

"I've been walking the route parallel to you, behind the crowd."

Sammie's heart gave a thump at his commitment to caring for her. "Clearly you were right to have worried. But I tell ya, this horse . . ." she said with wonder.

Alec patted and stroked Cedar's neck. "A mount you trust," he quoted Dr. Burk.

Sammie smiled down at him. "Yes. You chose wisely, Alec Neisson."

And so had she.

ALEC'S FINGERTIPS TINGLED with residual adrenaline as he shifted his attention from the blessedly unflappable Cedar and his precious cargo to the other horses from the A Bar H and their riders. Because they, too, had been well trained, after their initial frights, the horses had responded to the women's commands and allowed the helpful spectators to hold them. But it didn't mean they were happy about having to stand calmly when they clearly wanted to get as far away from the now-harmless and soggy string of lady finger firecrackers.

Pulling in several deep breaths to slow his heart rate and calm himself so the horses didn't pick up on the fear that had exploded through him when the firecrackers had first gone off, Alec approached Beth's mount.

The beautiful, midnight-black mare named Dahlia, undoubtedly chosen to be ridden by Beth because she perfectly matched Beth's dark hair, stood, blowing and quivering. A middle-aged man who obviously had experience with horses had a hold of the mare's bit while Beth leaned forward to stroke Dahlia's neck and coo to her.

Alec showed his thanks by patting the man on the shoulder, then moved to Beth. "You good?"

Beth smiled tremulously. "Just a tiny heart attack, but I'm good. Do me a favor and check her front left leg? She keeps pulling it up, and I can't tell if she's hurt or if it's just a nervous thing."

"Sure." Alec patted the horse on her shoulder. "Let's have a look, Dahlia." He ran his hands down her leg, applying gentle pressure. Dahlia didn't flinch away, but dutifully lifted her hoof when his hand reached her fetlock. Alec probed the area above the hoof and checked the hoof itself, but again, Dahlia didn't react.

Alec released the mare's leg and straightened. "I think she's fine. But if you think she's favoring it, just give me a shout. I'll be walking along with you guys for the rest of the route." This time in the street, between the crowd and the Buckin' Babes. No more lurking on the crowded sidewalk.

Justin appeared next to them, breathing hard from obviously running the couple of blocks that separated the staging area from where they were now on the relatively short parade route. "I heard the ruckus." He placed a hand on Beth's knee and studied her face. "Are you okay?"

"Yes. But Dahlia does not like firecrackers."

Justin smiled up at her, his relief obvious. "Few horses

do."

Leaving Beth to Justin's care, Alec moved on to Emma and her mount, a tall sorrel mare named Aubrey, with a flaxen mane and tail. Stress sweat glistened on the mare's reddish coat, and she danced from side to side, despite having her bridle held by yet another horse-savvy bystander.

Emma did not appear flustered at all.

Alec raised his brows at her.

Her grin widened. "That was fun."

Alec shook his head and moved on to Laura and Meira, whose mounts were standing nose to tail, as if watching each other's six. Alec circled them, making sure neither horse had nicked a leg with the edge of a hoof or was favoring anything.

He checked in with the women. "How are you two?"

Laura answered, "We're okay. Sammie?"

Alec looked to where Sammie had ridden Cedar near Emma to help calm Aubrey down. "She's just fine."

Meira let out a sigh of relief. "Thank goodness."

Laura asked, "Did anyone see which yahoo threw the firecrackers?"

Dearly wishing he knew the answer to that question, Alec shook his head. "Not that I've heard."

The same woman with the clipboard that Alec had noticed earlier hurried up to them. Speaking to Laura and Meira, she said, "Excuse me, I'm sorry about that . . . that disturbance." She waved a hand in the direction of the spent string of firecrackers that an older gentleman was in the processes of kicking to the curb with the side of his boot.

She huffed her disgust. "I don't know what gets into people. Anyway, do you think your horses are settled enough to continue? We still have one band left to walk and, of course, a small herd of longhorns to drive down Main Street to signal the official start of the rodeo."

Laura said, "Oh, of course. I think we're okay to continue, but let me check." Laura looked toward her partners, raised a hand, and called out, "Grit and Grace, we good?"

Meira nodded and Emma, Beth, and Sammie raised a hand in response and called back, "We're good."

Laura looked back down at the woman with the clipboard. "We'll continue on. Sorry about the delay."

The woman clutched her clipboard to her chest. "No, I'm sorry. Thank you so much."

Meira reined her mount around and walked her horse toward Emma, Beth, and Sammie who were reforming their line.

Laura shifted her attention to Alec. "You planning on staying close?"

Alec gave her a sharp nod. "Yes, ma'am."

Laura let out a breath. "Thank you." She clicked to her mount and headed for the other ladies.

Intending to stay not just close, but vigilant, Alec gave a quick, sharp whistle to catch Justin's attention. When the ranch manager looked to him, Alec pointed at Justin, then at the opposite side of the street. He then indicated that he would walk along the near side of the street. On the side closest to Sammie and Cedar. Even though the horse had proven himself trustworthy, with both he and Justin flanking the women and acting as their personal escorts as they rode and waved, hopefully, any other shenanigans would be discouraged.

Especially anything that could further put Sammie and the baby she carried in danger.

Just the thought of harm coming to the woman and child he now firmly thought of as his future filled Alec with a fear that surpassed even a bull's hoof coming at his face.

Chapter Fifteen

BACK IN THE horse stable at the A Bar H later that day, Alec took charge of returning Cedar to his stall, despite Sammie's willingness to help. When they'd arrived back at the A Bar H and begun to unload the horses from the fifth-wheel horse trailer, Alec had wanted Sammie to go rest up at the main house after being in the saddle all day. Thankfully, there hadn't been any other firecrackers thrown or further mischief. But the woman was stubborn. She trailed behind as he led the gelding into the coolness of the air-conditioned stable. He intended to give the very good horse a double helping of grain and an extra-long rubdown.

Alec suspected the other horses would receive similar treatment from their riders, with each woman insisting on unloading their mount from the horse trailer and leading them to their stalls.

Justin busied himself returning the saddles and bridles to the tack room while Carlos moved Justin's truck and the multi-horse trailer over to the bronc barn. It would be needed the next day when they transported the Grit and

Grace broncs to the rodeo grounds for the women to ride in their exhibition.

While the former Buckin' Babes' appearance at the Last Stand Rodeo's parade ultimately was a success, things could have gone very differently. Thanks to Cedar's unflappability, despite having a sting of firecrackers tossed right under his nose, Sammie had never been in danger. And the excellent horsemanship of the other women kept them from disaster.

In a way, the added excitement was a nice warm-up to their bronc riding exhibition scheduled for the day after tomorrow.

Alec led Cedar into his stall and unclipped the lead line. Sammie entered the stall after them, a curry brush in hand. When Alec stepped by her to get Cedar's grain, he couldn't resist running his hand along her amazing backside, his fingers tracing the curve just below her rhinestone encrusted jeans pocket.

She sent him a sidelong glance that set his blood humming. If they had been alone in the stable, Cedar would have had to wait for his extra grain treat. Maybe he could convince her to linger in Cedar's stall until the others left. Not only did he want an opportunity to show Sammie how important she was to him, but he also wanted to tell her as much. He'd decided, while walking the remainder of the parade route next to her and seeing all the happy families enjoying the day, that he wanted to make a real family with her and their child.

He was in love with her. And it was time he told her.

His gut churned with uncertainty. Did she return his feelings? He'd soon find out.

Returning to Cedar's stall with an almost full feed bucket, Alec called out to no one in particular, "Has it been decided which Grit and Grace broncs you all will ride for the exhibition?"

Emma's head appeared over the door to Aubrey's stall. "I'm riding Willie Bite."

"I call dibs on Betty Won't," Beth said from somewhere within Dahlia's stall.

Laura stepped out of the grain room, a bucket of grain in one hand. "Yo, Justin."

Justin emerged from the tack room, a bridle in one hand and a rag in the other. "Yeah?"

"You know the rest of the broncs better than we do, so which ones do you think Meira and I should ride?" Laura asked.

Justin cocked his head to one side, considering. "Depends on what sort of ride you want, and which horse is feeling it this week." He quickly stepped back into the tack room to hang up the bridle, then reemerged. "Let's go check them out now so you can take a practice ride tomorrow."

"Sounds good," Laura said. She hung the grain bucket in her horse's stall.

Meira stepped from the end stall. "Can someone get Dakota's grain?"

Alec quickly said, "I'll get it. Go."

Emma emerged from Aubrey's stall. "I'm coming too."

Beth called, "I'll go up to the house and get dinner going."

Sammie paused brushing the girth strap marks from Cedar's coat, and Alec could tell she was about to say she'd go with Beth to help with dinner, but Alec stopped her with a raised finger and a suggestive grin.

Sammie's eyebrows went up, but she remained silent.

Waiting for the others to leave, Alec gave Dakota his grain. He used the time to silently rehearse his declaration of love to Sammie. How he'd fallen for her at the rodeo in Pineville. How the baby is simply a bonus addition to the family he wanted to make with her. Hopefully, back in Oregon.

After making certain they were alone with the saddle horses, Alec headed back toward Cedar's stall, where he could see Sammie's black hat and blonde hair moving with each stroke of the curry brush. He'd come up behind her, wrap his arms around her, and whisper his love in her delectable ear.

His cell phone rang.

Finally, Drew was getting back to him. Alec pulled his phone from his pocket and checked the caller's name on the screen out of habit.

Wright, Thomas.

His grandfather, not his brother, was calling him.

His heart rate ticked up. He hadn't yet secured the roughstock contract for next year's rodeo here in Last Stand. He'd been too distracted. Not exactly how he'd intended to prove himself to his grandfather. As tempting as simply letting the call go to voicemail, then waiting to return the call when he had good news to give his grandfather was, Alec didn't dare. One did not ignore a phone call from Thomas Wright.

Turning away from the woman responsible for his distraction, Alec connected the call and placed the phone to his ear.

"Grandpa, hey!" Alec said, hopefully not too brightly.

"Alec." His grandfather had a way of putting all his expectations and disappointments together in one name. "You were in the Last Stand Rodeo parade today."

It hadn't been a question. Thomas Wright had a knack for knowing things.

Alec started to sweat. "Yes, sir." Thinking of the camera crew taping them, and what he and Sammie had been recorded doing, he tightened his grip on the phone. He'd really wanted to break the news of Sammie's pregnancy to Drew first, so Alec would know how best to tell the rest of the family. Just to be sure, he asked, "Did you see a news clip?"

"No. Gene Bauer called me."

"Gene called you?" Alec blurted, then turned back to face Sammie. She was standing in the opening of Cedar's stall, the curry brush hanging seemingly forgotten in her hand.

"He did. He said you hadn't gotten back to him with answers to the questions he had regarding which bulls the Wright Ranch would commit to sending to Last Stand for next year's rodeo."

Alec had spoken to Ian that night at the saloon, but he hadn't relayed what his oldest brother had told him to Gene and the other rodeo officials. He'd been interrupted, then thoroughly derailed by the woman watching him now with what he could only call suspicion.

He knew better than to try to explain himself. "No, sir. I'm afraid I haven't yet." He turned and walked away from Sammie. This subject would not help him convince her to return to Oregon with him. "I'll call Gene tonight and see if I can meet with him and the other rodeo officials to discuss next year's contract."

"No need. I secured the contract last month. Gene simply wants the names of the bulls I'll be sending so he can promote the lineup and entice some of the top-tier bull riders."

Alec froze. He'd thought his grandfather needed him to get the contract for the Wright Ranch. "You already have the contract? Why am I here, then?"

"Experience is never a bad thing, Alec. Checking out the A Bar H and Last Stand was a good use of your downtime while your shoulder heals. Confirm Last Stand has acceptable systems in place for the rough stock during their rodeo this year, then report back to me when you get home."

With frustration strangling him, Alec couldn't get a word in before his grandfather ended their call. He choked out a curse and turned around.

Sammie was gone.

HER VISION BLURRED by unshed tears that weren't going to remain unshed for long, Sammie all but ran out of the stable into the hot Texas evening. While at first she'd been stunned by what she heard Alec say to his grandfather, that the roughstock contract for next year's Last Stand Rodeo had always been his, it hadn't taken long for fury to take over. Then fear for her and her partners' future. All quickly eclipsed by heartbreak.

"Sammie!" Alec called after her, but there was no way she was going to stop. She never wanted to talk to him again.

Why had she thought she could ever compete with Thomas Wright? She had never been in contention. Grit and Grace had never had a chance at the contract. And Gene Bauer had used the chance for bidding on a contract he'd already awarded to someone else as a carrot to get her friends to fill his empty exhibition act slot in this year's rodeo.

Fury roared to the top of the rampaging emotions consuming Sammie. She slammed her way through the main house's back gate. She'd tell her friends about Gene Bauer's bullshit manipulation and convince them to back out. No way should the partners in Grit and Grace give the Last Stand Rodeo officials the satisfaction of having a Buckin' Babe-esque exhibition.

Of course, she would also have to tell them how she'd utterly failed doing the job she'd been so certain she could do. That she hadn't been taken seriously at all.

Shame swam to the top of the surging mass, and she paused outside the door to the mudroom. In the exact spot Alec had kissed her just the other night.

Despite memories such as standing in the moonlight right here with Alec, she loved it here at the A Bar H. She didn't want to give up on, or worse, be asked to leave Grit and Grace. There had to be a way for her to fix this.

Maybe she shouldn't tell the other girls just yet. Maybe she could hunt down Gene Bauer tomorrow and convince him to reconsider awarding next year's contract to the Wright Ranch. Especially after essentially lying to her to get the women to ride this year.

And who knows? Maybe the chance to showcase the bucking quality of the broncs from Grit and Grace the women would be riding might help their case and change Gene's mind.

A tentative hope calmed the storm within her as she let herself into the mudroom. While she would probably never forgive Alec, whether he was a part of it all or not, just out of principle, she could still achieve her dream of being a part of something where she actually mattered. And not just because she was pretty.

The sound of Beth's excited squeal reached her, and she followed the happy noise through the mudroom to the kitchen. Beth was holding a head of broccoli and standing in front of the small, flat-screen TV mounted above a desk nook in the kitchen.

Beth caught sight of Sammie and waved the broccoli at the TV. "We made the news today." She grabbed up the TV remote and rewound the program a bit. "Look!" She hit play.

Sammie moved to stand beside Beth as the professional camera crew's video, combined with cell phone footage from the parade, played on the screen. They'd compiled video of the former Buckin' Babes signing autographs and taking selfies with fans before the parade intercut with the firecrackers exploding directly in front of their horses.

The reporter commented on their expert horsemanship and how they were able to prevent possible tragedy. The segment ended with a clip of Sammie, mounted on Cedar, leaning down to kiss Alec. Text at the bottom of the screen read: *Samantha Abel receives good luck kiss from pro bull rider Alec Neisson.*

Beth made the squealing noise again and elbowed Sammie. "So cute!" Then she gasped. "Oh, shoot! I need to record this so the others can watch it." Beth handed Sammie the head of broccoli and started pushing buttons on the remote.

Sammie silently groaned and stared at the fat stalk of broccoli. Great. Now all the Texas Hill Country would know she had a thing going with Alec Neisson.

More than a thing. She was pregnant with his baby.

Whether it was from the smell of the fresh broccoli or simply a culmination of everything that had happened today, but Sammie suddenly felt very nauseous.

She thrust the broccoli back at Beth. "Sorry. Sick."

"Oh, sweetie," Beth said sympathetically.

Sammie hurried past her toward her room.

Beth called after her, "Do you need me to hold your hair?"

"Nope. Thanks." Just the fact that Beth offered brought the tears back to Sammie's eyes.

She'd do anything to keep from losing her friendship with these women.

THE NEXT MORNING Sammie woke later than usual, having struggled to sleep, her mind repeatedly playing out scenarios in which she convinced the Last Stand Rodeo officials to give next year's contract to Grit and Grace instead of the Wright Ranch. And, alternately, where she failed so spectacularly that she was asked to give up her ownership share in Grit and Grace and to leave the A Bar H.

Though she'd finally fallen asleep before dawn, she'd

eventually woken to a spectacular case of morning sickness. Wanting nothing more than plain crackers and weak tea, Sammie shuffled from her room toward the kitchen, still in the lounge pants and T-shirt she'd slept in. She'd hunt down the rodeo officials later.

She stopped short when she reached the kitchen. Instead of the kitchen and the breakfast nook being empty, as she'd expected, it was full of people. Sammie's gaze landed first on Alec, leaning against the counter with his arms and ankles crossed. His expression was inscrutable. Beth and Meira were bustling around the kitchen, pouring and delivering cups of coffee to Emma and Laura, who sat at the breakfast table with . . .

Sammie froze. Her grandmother, Barbara "Babs" Abel, was holding court in the A Bar H breakfast nook. Though only sixty—both Babs and Sammie's mom had been teenage mothers—Babs had never believed in using sunscreen or wearing a hat and obviously still favored the worst shade of brassy blonde to dye her piled-high hair.

When she spotted Sammie, Babs gave her a loving, grandmotherly look Sammie could honestly say she'd never seen before from the woman who'd raised her. "Well, look who decided to finally get up. Our little mother. Come here and give your g-ma a kiss, Samantha," Babs cooed, spreading her arms wide.

A boulder-size mass of dread landed with a thud in Sammie's already tumultuous gut.

Babs knew.

Moving on autopilot, Sammie went to her grandmother and bent for a kiss on the cheek. The combination of hairspray and potent perfume made Sammie's gag reflex go nuts.

Beth appeared at her side, holding out a plate of plain toast. Sammie nearly burst into tears of gratitude as she took the plate. Moving a step back from Babs, she started eating the toast in an attempt to settle her stomach.

Eyeing her, Babs said, "I was just telling these lovely friends of yours how I saw you and your beau on TV last night, and when I realized how close you were to me now, I had to get in my car and come see you. Even though it was a three-hour drive." She said it as if she'd had to trek across the Amazon to get here.

Laura said guiltily, "I congratulated her for becoming a great-grandmother."

Beth whispered, "We thought she knew."

Babs waved as regal a hand as possible with bright-yellow press-on nails. "While I would have loved to have heard it from my girl, it was such a lovely surprise. Especially knowing who your baby daddy is." She smiled her barracuda smile at Alec before taking a sip of her coffee.

Sammie glanced at Alec, but his face remained unreadable.

Nausea straight-up replaced the dread in the pit of her stomach.

Babs ran a finger along the corner of her mouth as if worried one drink of coffee might muss her coral lipstick. "Of all the things for this one—" She tilted her head at Sammie. "To finally listen to me about, I never thought it would be my advice to get knocked up by a handsome, rich man."

Sammie closed her eyes and prayed for the floor to open up and swallow her into oblivion.

Chapter Sixteen

NEEDING AIR, ALEC turned on his heel and left the kitchen. He exited the main house through the mudroom and banged his way through the gate in the fence surrounding the backyard and pool area. His angry stride ate up the space between the house and the bronc barn. He needed something to do, something to keep him busy enough to tamp down the storm of emotion churning inside him.

He'd stood there, in that kitchen, waiting for Sammie to open her eyes and deny what Babs Abel had said, but she hadn't. And when Beth had taken charge and guided Sammie from the room, Alec had just stood there, wondering what he was supposed to do. What was he supposed to think?

He entered the bronc barn feeling sucker punched. All his life he'd been raised to be careful, to be conscious of the fact that unscrupulous people would do anything to find a way to access the kind of wealth his grandfather and the rest of the family had accumulated through hard work and good decisions. Hell, even his own bull riding career had been successful enough to allow him to pay cash for a new truck if he needed it.

But what did he go and do? He fell in love with, and impregnated, a woman who'd been raised to trap a man. More specifically, a rich man.

Grabbing a brush, Alec went into Willie Bite's stall and began grooming the big gelding as the horse munched on a flake of hay.

Had Sammie really purposefully become pregnant to trap him? She certainly hadn't acted like a woman on a mission to trap a man.

Just the opposite.

Except when they'd first met. The minute she'd found out who he was, she was all flirt and sass. But hadn't he been, too, in his own way?

Alec set the brush aside and grabbed a hoof pick. He turned his back to Willie's head and picked up the horse's left front hoof, settling it between his knees so he could clean out the underside.

Why hadn't she simply denied what her grandmother said if it wasn't true? Why just stand there, eyes closed, like a kid who'd been caught stealing?

Alec dug at a clod of dried manure stuck in Willie's hoof. Without warning, Willie swung his head around and bit Alec on the butt. Not too hard, but enough to let him know he should have been more focused on what he was doing.

"Sorry, buddy," Alec said to the bronc and dropped his hoof. Maybe now wasn't the time to be working around big animals with teeth and a penchant for using them. He set the hoof pick on top of the stall door.

His cell phone buzzed in the opposite pocket from the one Willie had just taken a nip of.

Hoping Sammie was calling with her denial, Alec yanked his phone out and checked the screen. It was Drew, finally calling Alec back. He answered.

"'Bout time, Drew."

"Sorry, Alec. We had two bad wrecks last night. One bull rider and one bronc rider."

Alec rubbed his backside and eyed Willie. "I get that."

"What's up? You sounded like it's urgent."

The knot of warring emotions cinched tighter in Alec's gut. "It's a lot of things."

"Such as?" Concern threaded through Drew's voice.

Heaving a sigh, Alec quipped, "How much time do you have?"

"As much as you need," Drew said in a firm tone. "Shoot."

Alec decided to start with the least shocking development. "You know how I thought Grandpa was sending me here to Last Stand, Texas, to check out the A Bar H because he agreed to give rough stock to Grit and Grace?"

"And thus, forcing you to rest your dislocated shoulder, yes."

Alec automatically tested out the jacked-up shoulder in question. Surprisingly, it was feeling better. "Right. Anyway, once I was down here, he called, wanting me to negotiate a deal for the Wright Ranch to supply the rough stock for next year's Last Stand Rodeo. I was all excited, thinking he was giving me a chance to prove myself."

"But..."

Anger, tinged with resentment, sprung free of the knot of feelings battling for dominance inside him. "He'd already secured the contract. It's a done deal."

"I'm sorry, Alec. But you know how Grandpa is." Drew understood that showing their grandfather what he could do was important to Alec.

Straightening his cowboy hat on his head, Alec forced himself to focus and said, "That's really not why I wanted to talk to you."

"Okay."

Alec moved back to Willie's side, smoothing a hand over the big horse's withers. "You remember Peyton's friend, Sammie, right?"

"The real reason you hightailed it down to Texas? Yeah, I remember her."

Alec rolled his eyes and rested an elbow on Willie's back. Drew always had known Alec best. As the youngest siblings and relatively close in age, they had bonded tightly after their mother's accident. They'd comforted each other as well as caused mischief together. "Right. Turns out it was a good thing I came down here because Sammie is five weeks pregnant."

Drew made a distinct choking sound. "Five—so the baby is yours."

Drew had always been good at math. A good trait for a doctor. "Gold star for you, Dr. Drew." Alec pulled in a shuddering breath. "The thing is, I found out this morning, from Sammie's grandmother, that she'd been raised to trap a *handsome, rich man* by getting pregnant."

Drew was silent for a moment. "By trapping, I assume that means marriage?"

Alec shrugged, watching Willie yank another mouthful of hay from his wall-mounted feeder. "I guess. Babs didn't exactly say that, though."

Drew made a noise. "Babs?"

"Yeah. That's what Sammie's grandmother introduced herself as."

"Do you think what *Babs* said is true?" Drew was using what Alec thought of as his doctor's voice.

"I don't know what to think." Clearly, based on his inability to recognize his grandfather's intentions, Alec wasn't great at picking up on people's motivations.

"How did you find out she was pregnant?"

Alec thought back to the day the women of Grit and Grace had invited potential investors to the ranch and he'd taken the opportunity to corner Sammie, wanting an explanation for why she'd ghosted him. "She told me when I showed up here at Asher's ranch."

"Hmm. She didn't call you, or seek you out?"

She'd claimed she'd intended to call him, but she hadn't. "No. As a matter of fact, she'd ghosted me." And it had hurt more than just his pride.

"That doesn't sound like the actions of a woman looking to trap a man, either into marriage or child support."

The tightness in Alec's chest began to loosen. Drew's words seeped in and had Alec thinking. "And she told me no when I asked her to marry me."

"Wait, she said no when you were willing to do the right thing?" Now Drew was using his *my little brother is an idiot* voice.

Alec stepped away from Willie and ran a hand over his face. "Your little brother *is* an idiot."

His amusement clear, Drew said, "You said it, not me. But I think it's safe to say Sammie and Grandma Babs aren't on the same page."

Alec rubbed his face. "You're right, of course. Sammie has tried to keep me at arm's length. The only thing she cares about is getting next year's roughstock contract—"

"For the rodeo Thomas Wright has already buttoned up."

The tightness returned to Alec's chest. "Yeah."

"Is the contract signed?"

"I'm not sure. But I don't think so. They had questions about which bulls Grandpa was going to include in the deal."

"What are you going to do?"

"I don't know. Maybe try to convince the officials down here to give the contract to Grit and Grace instead?"

"That might cost you with Grandpa."

"You're right. But you know, I think I'm okay with it, though. I like it down here, Drew. These ladies are putting together something special with their Grit and Grace Rodeo Roughstock Company. They just need a little help."

"Will their rough stock be ready by next summer?"

"Their broncs are ready now, but their bull program will need work."

"Hmm. What about Sammie? Were you really only doing the right thing when you asked her to marry you?"

"No, I wasn't. I fell in love with her back in Pineville. But she thinks I'm only asking because of the baby."

"More proof Grandma Babs is full of crap. You need to convince her you want *her*, Alec."

"Simple enough," Alec said with as much sarcasm as he could muster. The way he'd hightailed it out of the house had to have left Sammie believing he was leaving for good. Leaving her.

"You might be an idiot, but one thing you don't lack is charm. So charm her, buddy. And hey, Alec?"

"Yeah?"

"Congratulations."

Alec grinned as determination slid into place within his

heart. "Thanks, man."

"Good luck, and let me know how it turns out."

"Thanks, Drew. I will."

Alec ended the call with his brother, the weight lifting off his chest. He planted his hands on his hips and considered the big bronc who was eyeing him as he munched his hay. "What do you think, Willie? Maybe I should take a page out of your book and just bite Sammie in the butt to get her attention."

The horse gave Alec a slow blink that he took as a yes.

THE COWARD SHE was, Sammie hid in her room until lunchtime, only half-faking the fact she was sick. While she'd allowed Beth to bring her more plain toast, she'd refused the other women's offers of help or sympathy. Even when Babs had knocked to say she was heading back to their little town of Bellmead, but would be keeping in touch, Sammie had groaned a response and buried her head beneath her pillow.

Sammie had never felt more miserable in her life. The thought that Alec believed she would sink so low as to trap him by becoming pregnant with his baby absolutely broke her heart. She really had begun to believe they could find a way to come together, maybe even as a family.

But now, after he'd stood silent in the kitchen after Babs pronounced as fact something that wasn't true at all, then he'd turned and left without so much as a word, Sammie was having to come to grips with the idea she'd lost Alec.

The man she now realized, without a shadow of a doubt, that she loved.

Her future would consist of just her and her child. And her friends here at Grit and Grace. If she could convince them to let her and the baby stick around, that is. To accomplish that, she needed to get her butt up off her bed and go to the rodeo grounds and find Gene Bauer.

Somehow, someway, she needed to convince him to give them the contract.

Sammie was dressed, noticing for the first time her favorite dark-wash sparkly jeans were growing tight, with her hair and makeup done, when a knock sounded on her bedroom door.

"Sammie?" It was Meira. "You feeling up to coming with us to the rodeo?"

Sammie pulled open the door, her answer in her appearance.

Meira's beautiful face relaxed into a smile. "Oh good. The guys are loading the broncs and the rest of us are getting out the gear."

Sammie grabbed her phone and stepped from the room. "I can help."

Meira steered her toward the kitchen. "You probably should eat something first. Beth made you what she called a bland, but hearty, turkey sandwich. It's in the fridge."

Sammie's heart squeezed in her chest. She loved her friends. "That's really sweet," she said as she fetched the sandwich. Beside the plastic wrap-covered plated sandwich was a full glass of milk. Sammie's vision swam.

Meira snagged her hat and chaps from a chair and headed for the back door. "Come on down when you're done eating."

Sammie signaled she would with the chilled glass of milk. Standing at the sink to eat the sandwich, she couldn't help but wonder if Alec was one of the guys loading the broncs. She hoped so. It hurt too much to think he'd already gone.

EMMA WAS THE final former Buckin' Babe to ride in the Last Stand Rodeo's opening night exhibition. Sammie leaned down into the chute, holding the thick, braided rein attached to Willie Bite's halter as Emma eased down into her saddle. Sammie gave Emma the rein, then took hold of Emma's protective vest, ready to haul her to safety if Willie tried to stack her up against the front wall of the chute.

So far, the women had ridden well. More importantly, as far as Sammie was concerned, the broncs they had brought with them were putting on a rank bucking clinic. Sammie couldn't be prouder.

Justin had been pulling the flank strap for the Grit and Grace's broncs, but he stepped away and Alec took his place.

Thus far, Sammie had been able to avoid him. She'd been relieved to find him still at the A Bar H and hadn't questioned his willingness to help with the broncs and the women's gear as they readied for their exhibition ride. They'd ridden in separate vehicles to the rodeo grounds, and in the bustle of getting the broncs into their holding pen and the women's gear ready, there hadn't been a moment to speak.

She'd noticed he was even wearing a Grit and Grace-logoed western shirt instead of the Wright Ranch one he'd worn when meeting with the rodeo officials.

He caught her looking at the embroidered logo again. "Justin loaned me one. I think it looks better on me, don't you?" His smile was cheeky.

Her heart thumped in response. "I do."

His expression grew serious. "It's okay, Sammie. We're okay."

Her heart started to pound. "Wha—?"

From in the chute, Emma said, "Hey, you lovebirds, I've got fifteen hundred pounds of raring-to-go bronc here. How 'bout you kiss and make up later?"

Alec's grin came back. "Just waitin' on a nod, Emma."

She leaned way back in the saddle, raised the rein high, then gave a very exaggerated nod. The cowboy in charge of pulling the chute gate open from within the arena responded by yanking the gate open in the same breath that Alec pulled tight the flank strap, fitted around the horse's trunk just in front of his hind legs.

Willie Bite erupted sideways into the arena, proving once again he was indeed born to buck. Emma rode him with flare, but unlike the exhibition ride she'd given for the potential investors at the A Bar H, she was legitimately bucked off six seconds into her eight-second ride.

The crowd cheered her with as much enthusiasm as they had for the other women ranch bronc riders.

As soon as she was certain Emma hadn't been hurt by the buck off, Sammie whooped and jumped up and down. She turned to Alec, who opened his arms to her.

Sammie hesitated, but Alec grabbed her up into an embrace, knocking their hats askew.

Pressing his mouth to her ear so he'd be heard over the noise of the rodeo arena, Alec said, "I love you, Sammie. I don't care about the hows or the whys. I want to be with you. I want to make a family with you and our baby."

Sammie didn't know whether to laugh or cry. He didn't believe her grandma? Or he didn't care whether Sammie had supposedly trapped him or not? What about his family? She wanted this, wanted him, but there were still so many obstacles . . . "But in Oregon, right?"

He released her enough for her to step back, but snagged hold of her hand. "We need to talk."

An understatement if she'd ever heard one. She nodded her agreement, fighting the tears gathering in her throat. They started off the catwalk above the bucking chutes, but

Gene Bauer met them on his way up the stairs.

"Just the people I wanted to see," Gene said. He moved back down the stairs, encouraging Sammie and Alec to follow. "Those Grit and Grace broncs are amazing. I'd heard they were good, but they performed exceptionally here at the rodeo."

Pride swelled in Sammie's chest. "Thank you, Mr. Bauer."

"Please, call me Gene. Now, I just made a few phone calls, and I have a proposition for you. What would you say to splitting the roughstock contract for next year? You, meaning the Wright Ranch . . ." He pointed to Alec. "Will supply the bulls. And you . . ." He aimed his finger at Sammie. "Will supply the broncs."

Alec squeezed her hand. Hope, with a chaser of excitement, flooded her. "And the steers. Grit and Grace has loads of amazing steers." At least they would by this time next year.

Gene considered it for a moment. "Done. The local contractor will supply broncs and steers."

Alec said, "I'll have to clear it with my grandfather."

Gene shook his head. "Already spoke to Thomas. He agrees it's an equitable division."

Sammie had to fight to contain a squeal of happiness. At least one thing was working out.

Stepping away, Gene said, "We'll talk in the coming week. I have a rodeo to run right now."

"Of course," Sammie gushed. "Thank you, Gene."

As Gene walked away, Alec took hold of Sammie's other hand and met her gaze. "That takes care of one problem."

"Alec, it's massive! Grit and Grace has their first contract." She'd done it. She hadn't let her friends down, after all.

"I still have a proposition for you."

The riot of happiness and excitement calmed in an instant. "What?"

"Marry me, Samantha Abel. Not because you're having my baby. Because I love you, and I think you love me too. We'd have an amazing life together."

Her heart stalled. "In Oregon," she stated. "I can't—"

"No. I'd like to stay here, with you, at the A Bar H. If the partners of Grit and Grace will have me, I'd like to help with getting the bull training and breeding program up and running."

Behind them, Laura said, "Oh, we'll have you."

Sammie turned and found Laura, Meira, and Beth descending the stairs from the chute catwalk, obviously having heard what Alec said.

Emma appeared around the scaffolding, brushing the arena dirt from her backside. "Have what?"

Bouncing on her toes, Beth said, "Alec is asking Sammie if he can stay here with her and work for us."

Emma's eyes went wide. "And she's hesitating? Say yes, you numbskull! Don't let that crunchy ol' Babs keep you from finding true love."

Sammie looked into Alec's blue eyes, darkened by what she had to acknowledge as love. Her heart pounded in her throat. "I really didn't want to prove her right."

Alec's mouth curled upward. "You won't be because you didn't trap me. I willingly want to spend the rest of my life with you. Do you want to spend the rest of your life with me, Samantha?"

Sammie swayed toward him. "Yes. Yes, I do. I will marry you, Alec Neisson. Because I love you too." She raised up to kiss him, but stopped a breath away, a smile pulling at her mouth. "But don't call me Samantha."

The End

If you enjoyed *All's Fair in Love and Rodeo*, you'll love the other books in….

Grit and Grace series

Book 1: *All's Fair in Love and Rodeo*

Book 2: *Catching a Christmas Cowboy*

Available now at your favorite online retailer!

More Books by Leah Vale

The Rodeo Romeos series

Book 1: *The Bull Rider's Second Chance*

Book 2: *Wrangling the Cowboy's Heart*

Book 3: *The Cowboy's Vow*

Book 4: *The Cowboy Doctor*

Available now at your favorite online retailer!

About the Author

Having never met an unhappy ending she couldn't mentally "fix," Leah Vale believes writing romance novels is the perfect job for her. A Pacific Northwest native with a B.A. in Communications from the University of Washington, she lives in Central Oregon, with a huge golden retriever who thinks he's a lap dog. While having the chance to share her "happy endings from scratch" is a dream come true, dinner generally has to come premade from the store.

Thank you for reading

All's Fair in Love and Rodeo

If you enjoyed this book, you can find more from all our great authors at TulePublishing.com, or from your favorite online retailer.

Made in the USA
Coppell, TX
06 April 2025